The Dragons of Incendium

WYVERN'S
WARRIOR

DEBORAH
COOKE

AUTHOR OF *WYVERN'S PRINCE*

ISBN: 978-1-927477-99-1

PROLOGUE

Gemma exchanged her vows with Venero in the palace of Incendium. When they had pledged to each other before the royal family, Kraw brought the great chalice filled with the purple brew for HeartKeepers and Venero drank half, then Gemma drained the cup. Her heart was filled to bursting with joy and the knowledge that Venero's child had already been conceived. They made the long-overdue alliance between the planets of Incendium and Regalia with their vows, and she couldn't wait to see the future they would build.

It wasn't an elaborate wedding with a long list of dignitaries in attendance. Gemma wasn't wearing a magnificent dress, just one of her favorites, and there weren't a dozen attendants in the procession. Her sisters were present, except for Drakina who had gone to Terra with Troy after Gemma's wedding to Urbanus, and Anguissa who was seldom home. Her parents were present, of course, as well as the royal retinue. Kraw beamed at her, as if he were her second father.

Venero's crown had to be secured in Regalia, but they had conceded one day to this celebration. Gemma's father, King Ouros of Incendium, had agreed to provide the troops she requested for the mission to Regalia and insisted upon leaving a sizable portion of them in service there until one year after Venero controlled the throne. Gemma was pleased that her old friend, Farquon, would command the assigned troops and report directly to Gemma and Venero.

Ouros' concession had been hard won. He had protested Gemma's departure for Regalia, fearing for her welfare. She hadn't told him that she'd conceived Venero's child already, but her father could probably smell the change in her scent. It had been her mother, Queen Ignita, who had argued for Gemma's choice, reminding her husband that a bride must make her future by her husband's side.

Gemma and Venero would depart for Regalia with an army the following morning.

Married.

Gemma turned from the chalice to accept congratulations, Venero's hand in hers, and found that a small table was being placed before them. Thalina placed a dark blue box upon the table with such care that Gemma guessed its contents.

"You made another one?" she asked, and Thalina nodded, her pride clear. "And you're giving it to us?"

Thalina nodded, her eyes dancing. "I hope you like it."

"I don't understand," Venero murmured but Gemma smiled at him.

"Thalina has learned to make automatons."

His eyes widened in surprise. "Really? That's impressive."

"And you haven't even seen this one yet," Flammara said.

"Touch the button," Thalina instructed, and Gemma did, pushing the large gold circle on the side closest to her. It looked like a seal, embossed with the insignia of Incendium, but actually was a button. It clicked when she pressed it and she stood back, waiting and watching.

Music began to tinkle. The box spun, then parted at the seams and fell open, revealing its deep orange interior. Nestled inside was a large egg with an iridescent surface, much like the natal egg of a dragon shifter but smaller. This egg was about half the size that Gravitas' egg had been. The patterns on its surface appeared to move, but Gemma looked closer. The surface of the egg had at least three layers, each a different color, the top two punctured in different patterns. The lower two spun in opposite directions, giving the illusion of the changing surface of a natal egg.

Her family caught their breath as one and gathered near to watch. Thalina was clearly brimming with anticipation.

"Wait for it," Flammara said, who must have seen the automaton before.

"Do I have to do anything else?" Gemma asked.

Thalina shook her head. "Let it do what it does."

"And prepare to be amazed," Flammara said.

A crack revealed itself in the surface of the egg, looking as if it started at the summit and spreading downward. Gemma knew the break had to have been designed into the egg's surface, but the illusion was remarkable. Parts of the egg's surface slid down inside the rest of the shell, dropping with irregular timing in an almost perfect echo of Gravitas' hatching.

"I wish Drakina could see this," Gemma whispered, entranced.

"She will, the next time she comes home," Thalina said. "It won't change."

"Part of the beauty of an automaton," Venero said quietly. "It's constant and predictable."

Thalina smiled.

A large piece of shell dropped inside and there was a croak, like the cry of a young dragon. As the rest of the shell dropped to make a kind of nest, wings rose from the interior. They were pale green and leathery, shaped exactly like those of infant dragons. Gemma smiled at the attention to detail—the nail at the tip of the wing was pale and looked soft, as it would on a newborn.

The wings moved slowly at first, then spread outward, as if with dawning confidence. The dragon sheltered inside the wings was revealed, its back studded with gems that caught the light and a line of iridescent feathers down its back. It was green and black and blue, marvelous in its detail. The head of the mechanical dragon lifted and it tipped its head back to make a second, louder cry. Gemma smiled at the red lining of its mouth and the tiny pearls placed like baby teeth.

Its wings beat harder and it rose out of the egg, appearing to stretch for the sky. Its tail coiled beneath its haunches, probably hiding a metal support. The music turned triumphant as a spiral of flame erupted from the dragon's mouth. Gemma realized the flame was a spinning tube of orange glass, artfully shaped. The dragon gave its last final victorious cry before lowering itself into the shell again and sheltering itself beneath its wings. The shell reassembled itself and the box folded up and spun once. The music fell silent when the gift looked as it had upon presentation.

"Well done!" King Ouros cried, leading the applause. He crossed the floor to give Thalina a kiss on the cheek. "You have learned much from Thantos the clockmaker." He shook hands with the beaming older gentleman from the village. Gemma had wondered why he was there. "Thank you, Thantos, for indulging the fascination of my daughter."

"The princess long ago exceeded my skills, your highness. She is a most apt student and might be a master clockmaker herself."

"If she desired a trade, that could be hers," Ouros agreed mildly, and Gemma knew he was thinking that

Thalina's future role would be greater than that of a tradesperson.

"I can have a skill without undertaking a trade," Thalina said, a new defiance in her tone. She'd always been the quiet one, but it seemed that triumph had given her new confidence. "And sooner or later, Father, Incendium must embrace reality."

Gemma winced, because she knew her father disliked being challenged before others.

"Scintillon's Law is irrevocable," Ouros said, his tone a little more stern. "And you know it, Thalina."

"It is also twelve hundred years old," Thalina countered. "I would hate for Incendium to become backward and primitive because of a refusal to update our policies."

Their father inhaled and his eyes glittered. "That will never happen, even without androids. Incendium remains in the upper echelons of successful empires."

"For how long?" Thalina challenged.

Father and daughter glared at each other and Gemma cleared her throat.

"Scintillon's Law," she said lightly, turning to Venero. "I assume you know of it?"

"The edict of the first King of Incendium that outlaws androids on any of the planets in the Fiero-Four system, including Incendium and Regalia." Her new husband nodded. "It's well-documented and included on the curriculum of legal courses about androids and cyborgs in the law schools of Advocia."

"So, we're already known to be backward and superstitious by the rest of the galaxy," Thalina said.

"You don't know that superstition was behind Scintillon's choice," Ignita said softly, obviously trying to make peace.

"It can't have been based on experience," Thalina argued. "Not twelve hundred years ago. Making laws based on assumptions and prejudices is backward."

Ouros was remarkably silent about this. In fact, he fired a quelling glance at his wife, one that intrigued Gemma.

"Perhaps not in this case, Thalina," Venero acknowledged. Gemma smiled, knowing he was going to sound like a lawyer. "In terms of statutes, Scintillon's Law has the beauty of simplicity. In outlawing androids, Scintillon ended all discussion of their rights and legal status in Incendium society before such conversation could even begin. They have no status except as illegal entrants, which makes them subject to export or decommission immediately upon identification of their nature." He nodded. "There are societies who find that simplicity enviable and even a mark of foresight."

"Because...?" Ouros invited.

"Because androids have been developed in those twelve hundred years which emulate sentience, and perhaps even possess it," Venero said. "That complicates the distinction between androids and biological organisms in those societies, particularly if the two aren't readily distinguishable."

"They'd have to be caught first," Thalina said.

"Exactly," Venero agreed.

"You mean androids like Arista," Gemma said and her husband nodded.

"Exactly. And where is the line between cyborgs and androids, as well as cyborgs and humans?" Venero mused, sounding even more like a lawyer. "Is the distinction in the original impulse? In the source of the mind governing the organism? In which system is ascendant? Is it in the percentage of the corpus that is biological versus mechanical? How are such questions to be reliably answered in a timely fashion? The questions are complicated, with ramifications that provoke more than a little envy for Incendium's law code."

Thalina rolled her eyes.

King Ouros beamed at this endorsement of his legacy. "And so there should be. We have built an advanced society without such creatures in our midst, are one of the greatest trading empires of the galaxy and one with a standard of living for our citizens in the top percentile. There is much reason for pride in this."

The family began to murmur to each other, and Gemma gave Thalina a kiss. "Thank you so much. It's just wonderful and will have pride of place in our home."

Thalina smiled. "I knew you'd like it."

"You must have been working on it for years," Gemma said."

"I was, but it's a perfect wedding gift, I think."

"It's incredible. You are skilled," Venero said and Gemma watched her sister blush.

"But I want to do more..." Thalina began.

"Don't put yourself on the wrong side of Scintillon's Law," Gemma advised, seeing exactly where her sister's thoughts were headed.

"There's no legal cause or precedent for appeal," Venero reminded her.

Thalina's lips set. "I can't believe you didn't know about Arista," she said to Gemma. "Couldn't you smell that she wasn't human?"

"No. I never guessed," Gemma admitted. "Only Venero knew."

"How?" Thalina asked.

"Because she didn't dream," Venero supplied. "If I hadn't tried to send her a dream, and had the ability to do so in the first place, I wouldn't have known, either."

"And neither of us guessed about Felice," Gemma said.

"Neither did I," Thalina sighed, her gaze fixed on the automaton. "It's amazing that they were so advanced. I wish I'd taken a closer look at your pet when I had the chance." Gemma saw the yearning in her sister's eyes. "I'd love to see an android again," she said softly. "I wouldn't miss a second chance."

"You'd just want to take it apart," Gemma teased.

"I'd want to know whether I could tell its nature," Thalina said, then smiled. "And then I'd want to take it apart." She turned to Ouros and raised her voice. "Will you send me to Cumae, Father? I could train as a Warrior Maiden, the way Gemma did."

"No," Ouros said flatly. "Such a course would be dangerous."

"It wasn't for Gemma!"

"You and Gemma have very different natures," their father said. "Gemma was always skilled at fighting and alert to her circumstance at all times. I knew that she would defend herself well on Cumae, regardless of what happened. You, however, can lose yourself in an intellectual puzzle, showing such focus that everything else in your vicinity becomes irrelevant to you. The same keen attention to detail that allowed you to create this marvel could be perilous to your survival." His brows rose. "And that means, my dear Thalina, that you will remain where I can ensure your protection, until the Carrier of your Seed is revealed. I hope that he proves himself worthy of becoming your HeartKeeper, but if not, you will remain beneath my care."

Thalina frowned, but had no chance to argue.

Their father managed the situation as he often did. He turned and raised his hands to the others, changing the subject in his royal way. "Let us applaud the cleverness of Thalina in creating this automaton and her generosity in giving it to Gemma and Venero as a wedding gift." The family clapped heartily. "Let us thank Thantos for his tutelage and his indulgence of a royal curiosity." The applause grew louder. Ouros turned to gesture at the automaton. "And let us watch this dragon hatch once again, before we descend to the great hall to dine and celebrate the marriage of Gemma and Venero!"

The family hooted and cheered, gathering closer as Gemma pushed the gold button one more time. Her thoughts were spinning, because she understood Thalina's frustration. Maybe she could convince Venero to take a trip outside their system and take Thalina along. Their father might allow Thalina to travel under her sister's protection, and Thalina could satisfy some of her curiosity.

It wasn't the right moment to make such a suggestion, but Gemma would watch and wait for it. She wanted all of her sisters to be as happy as she was, and once she was securely established as Queen of Regalia, she might be able to help to make that happen.

"First things first," Venero whispered, so obviously guessing her thoughts that Gemma smiled at him.

"Don't cheat," she advised.

He held his fingertips to his heart. "And provoke a dragon queen? I'm not that foolish." He caught her close and whispered in her ear. "But I don't need to peek into your thoughts. I know you because I love you. Let's secure our future, then see what we can do." He lifted one brow. "I just might have to go to Advocia for advice."

"I do love you," Gemma said with heat. The newly married pair kissed just as the automaton finished its sequence, much to the delight of the family surrounding them.

CHAPTER ONE

There were no dragons on Incendium.

Acion wasn't disappointed because he didn't have the programming for such an emotional reaction. He wasn't surprised, since he didn't have that capacity, either. All the same, he had a sense of something lacking.

That was new, so he analyzed it.

It was a strange awareness, unlike anything he's experienced before. It was so unusual that he couldn't even compare it to anything. (He tried.)

He walked through Incendium's capital city, seeking explanations in his vast datastores.

There was a fifty per cent probability that this reaction was due to the fact that he couldn't add to his log by investigating a life form he hadn't previously encountered. But still, it was illogical that he'd never experienced this sense of lack before. He'd been confronted with such situations many times in the past and had simply awaited new opportunities to add to his log.

There was a ninety-five per cent chance that this new experience was due to the enhanced programming that the Hive had insisted upon installing before Acion's departure on this mission. That would explain its novelty.

The notion satisfied Acion. He calculated a ninety-seven per cent probability that the Hive was testing this new software. That was logical. He existed to serve. Acion gave full rein to his newfound sense of incompletion, knowing that the data from his sensors could only help the Hive to continue to refine androids such as himself.

But where *were* the dragons? Incendium was ruled by a king who was a dragon shifter, who was married to a dragon shifter, and who had twelve dragon shifter daughters. Incendium had a population that was predominantly humanoid, but which also included about seven per cent dragon shifters. This information was in his brief. Given the number of people in Incendium's capital city, Acion found it reasonable that he should have seen at least one dragon. In fact, by his calculations, based on the number of humanoids he'd counted since leaving the starport, he should have seen forty-three.

But he hadn't.

Not one.

Oh, there were dragons on pennants, dragon-shaped jewelry, dragons embroidered on clothing and dragons in shop windows. He paused before one window, that of a clockmaker, his attention caught by a glittering display. The dragon flapped its wings and took flight, circling around a castle tower and breathing fire. The castle was about half Acion's height and the dragon could have sat on his hand.

The children on either side of him were clearly delighted, but Acion didn't understand. The dragon was made of metal. The "fire" was a twisting piece of orange glass, fixed in the dragon's mouth, which spun as the dragon "flew." The dragon was secured to a metal stick, which terminated in a track that circled the castle. It was mechanical and not a real dragon at all.

He considered that as an illusion, it was somewhat lacking. What was the appeal?

The children chattered to each other in their excitement, using the universal galactic tongue. Acion heard an inflection on the vowels, which must be the local variant, but knew he could mimic that well enough.

"Where are the real dragons?" he asked one child.

"You're not from here," the little boy declared, startling Acion with his conviction.

A most unexpected assertion, and one worthy of investigation. "How can you tell?" The boy's reply would help Acion to improve his ability to blend into local society.

Not that he would be on Incendium for long.

"Everyone *knows* they're in the palace," the boy said with scorn and pointed to the castle that loomed over the town. It was built of local stone cut into large blocks and constructed upon a natural hill. Acion knew this from his brief, but found that the actual castle appeared much larger than in the records he'd reviewed. The biggest dragon pennant he'd seen so far snapped in the wind above its high tower. It was deep blue with a golden dragon on it.

He recognized the colors and insignia of the reigning monarch, King Ouros.

High above the tower, Acion could detect the starport of Incendium in low orbit, with shuttles rising to it and descending from it. They appeared as lights in a line, moving slowly up or down. Just hours before, he'd been there himself. He'd rented a Starpod of his own, as instructed, in order to ensure that his own quick departure from Incendium city wasn't hampered and left it at the star station in Incendium city. He estimated that he would be at the port again within 9.4 local hours.

Acion realized the child was still watching him, waiting for a reply.

"Then I'll look there," he said and bowed to the little boy. The brief had said that bowing was important in

Incendium society, but Acion's move seemed to amuse the boy. "Thank you for your assistance." Acion turned to stride to the castle.

"Where *are* you from?" the boy called after him, but Acion ignored him.

That data was not available to that individual at that time.

It occurred to him he might have just spoken to a dragon shifter, who had chosen his humanoid form for the moment.

Acion reviewed the information provided to him. The dragon shifters of Incendium came of legal age at eighty-one Incendium years, but there was no clear information as to their age when they gained the ability to shift shape in the first place. He made a notation on the Incendium file in his memory, drawing attention to the missing detail, then continued onward.

What *was* this strange sense he felt? He might call it desire, but it wasn't sexual. He might call it a need, but it wasn't like his body's imperative for food or water or sleep. Acion searched the thesaurus in his databank and found a curiously apt word.

Yearn.

He tried it out. *He yearned to see a dragon.* That sounded true. It sounded right. It *felt* right, which was even more interesting. Acion nodded, satisfied by the Hive's modifications to his programming. What nuance. What subtlety. His reaction was almost organic.

What was the cost of the change? Would his other reactions, the ones that ensured his survival, be compromised?

Acion ran a check of his systems and found all operating at full capacity.

The Hive had called the modifications "enhancements." There was, after all, a ninety-seven per cent probability that Acion and his mission was a test of the effectiveness of these enhancements, whatever they were.

This was as it should be.

Acion existed to serve.

Thalina was in the chamber deep beneath her father's castle called the Vault, where the security system of the palace was monitored and where the processors were stored.

She was bored.

The processors in question were comparatively large, each being a cube two-hand-spans on a side. Thalina thought them ridiculous clumsy compared to the personal computers they all used, which were thin films that could adhere to any surface. She usually wore hers on the inside of her left forearm. There was no doubting the impressive power of the nine main processors. They controlled all the exits and entrances to the palace, as well as monitoring every window and door, external and internal. There were very few places in the palace that weren't monitored—the royal beds and lavatories were an exception. The processors also automatically backed up the data on every personal film in the palace at short, regular intervals and kept it all forever.

Despite the elegance and efficiency of the system, something was wrong.

Worse, King Ouros had been the one to notice it.

Because Thalina, his third daughter, had always been mechanically inclined, he'd invited her to join him in the chamber for the investigation. She would much rather have gone to the clockmaker in town to check his progress on his newest automaton, but she didn't protest. The new automaton was to be a gift for her father on the anniversary of his coronation, a collaboration between herself and the clockmaker, and intended to be a surprise. She didn't dare even think about it in her father's presence.

Thalina had been to the Vault before, so wasn't particularly interested in its contents. Her tutor had given her a challenge the year before, to identify the means by which an item entered the palace and left it again, so she'd spent a good bit of time in the Vault solving that riddle.

The three guards listened as her father explained the difficulty with his access to the secret passage that led from his personal office to the audience chamber. Ector, the Captain of the Guard, stood before her father, with two of his subordinates ensuring that the recordings in question were displayed at Ouros' command. They reviewed the recorded sequences of the king trying to open and seal the portal that very morning, and checked his access code.

It should have worked.

It hadn't worked.

They reviewed the sequence again and again and again, which showed her father to have been right—again and again and again—an exercise that pleased him enormously. Thalina, in contrast, found her toe tapping.

"Might I look at the gates?" she asked, wanting to have a glimpse of the bustling village instead of this utilitarian little room. One of the lower ranking guards indicated a viewing screen with a bow. "Have the codes changed?" she asked, knowing they must have been.

"On schedule, princess. Of course." The guard entered the new code, and Thalina watched him to memorize it. She had no intention of using it. It was just her nature to collect such information.

The screen was quickly filled with a display from the lowest gate, the one that allowed waste water to flow into the river. It was barred with a portcullis and metal mesh, naturally, which provided no obstacle to the water but a considerable barrier to anything larger than a mouse.

"It appears that the door unlocks then locks again before it can be opened," Ector said to her father.

"Exactly!" Ouros agreed. "This next time, I tried to grab it."

"But even you weren't quick enough, your highness. That is remarkable."

"And the mechanism?" asked another guard.

"It's oiled and perfectly operational, Father," Thalina supplied without turning around. "I checked it yesterday when you first complained about it."

"It seemed slower yesterday," her father explained.

"The issue has to be the computer controlling the latch," Thalina added.

"We shall see about that, princess," said Ector, clearly disliking the implication that any failure originated with the systems he monitored.

Thalina sighed, knowing she'd never be a diplomat. It was better to just be quiet. Definitely simpler. She toggled the display to the next gate. This one led to the small bailey behind the kitchens. Some eggs were being delivered and the cook was arguing over the price. Thalina yawned and moved on.

There were two knights riding through the main gate. The one on the right was rather handsome and looked familiar. Thalina magnified the image. It *was* Thierry, one of her father's favorite champions. A notorious flirt. Her sister Flammara was obsessed with Thierry, and he was audacious enough to encourage that princess's attention. He'd even ridden into tournament with Flammara's colors recently, at the Inter-Galactic Joust on Certamen, much to the disapproval of Ouros. Thalina doubted the flirtation would end well for Thierry if he continued to tempt fate.

Or the king.

She changed the display. Three astrologers were at the queen's gate, a smaller gate on one side of the palace and one that was more discreet. It looked as if one astrologer was Nero, the new arrival who Peri liked so well. Thalina didn't mind him, although she wished he'd hurry up and finish the charts of all the sisters he'd promised to do. That was probably her mother's fault, though. Ignita had appointed Nero to be her own astrologer and probably was monopolizing his time. Nero had an unusual method of casting a chart, one that gave different results and one that annoyed the senior members of the Royal College of Astrology like Astrum. Thalina liked him for that alone. He said he could chart when and where each princess would meet her HeartKeeper, which was enough to spark the curiosity of all the princesses, Thalina included.

She toggled the display. A merchant at the viceroy's door, looking for payment. Kraw was greeting him politely, so it was all routine. She yawned again and moved to the next portal.

And straightened. There was nothing routine about the man knocking at the main portal for admission. Thalina had never seen a man like him. It wasn't the way he was dressed, for he wore a white shirt with a dark tabard, dark chausses and dark boots like pretty much every other man in Incendium. His cape was plain and dark but looked heavy and warm. He didn't wear a hat and his head was shaved bald, which was unusual.

But best of all, he was tall and broad-shouldered, built strong like the warriors in her father's employ. Thalina guessed he was all muscle and a good fighter. There was something agile about his movements and she liked the glint in his eyes. He wasn't dumb, like many of the tournament fighters.

Like Thierry.

A very feminine bit of Thalina was intrigued.

Maybe he was a mercenary.

"I have a gift for the king," he said to the porter, his

deep voice devoid of inflection. "I will present it to him."

"The frack you will," the guard on duty there muttered, probably not realizing his words would be picked up by the monitoring system. He raised his voice. "I will require your identification and credentials, good visitor, before you can be admitted to the palace."

The arrival tugged off his gloves and offered his left hand, which had a screen embedded in the palm. How interesting. He probably wasn't from Incendium or another planet in the Fiero-Four system because such augmentations were suspect—given Scintillon's Law— and unfashionable. Thalina magnified the screen for a better look and managed to read the displayed words as they flashed.

His name was Acion.

He was from Cumae.

He closed his hand as the guard verified his information.

Cumae? Gemma had trained on Cumae and her best friend there and Sword Sister, Arista, had actually been an android. Gemma hadn't guessed, which said a great deal about the sophistication of the android in question.

Thalina was sure that Arista had fellow androids. No maker could create an android that sophisticated without having made more before.

Or even after.

Now that Acion had removed his gloves, Thalina glimpsed a blue tattoo under the silver ring on his right thumb. She tried to magnify the image to get a better look at the tattoo, but the movement of his hands and the ring obscured it.

Thalina changed the magnification to focus on Acion's face. His expression was bland, but his gaze was flicking. He had to be looking at the guard, the gate, the security measures. His eyes moved too quickly for a human.

Thalina felt a flutter of excitement.

Was his body augmented? Was he a cyborg?

Or was he another android?

Either way, Thalina wanted a better look at him and his functionality.

What was the gift he'd brought for her father? Could she meet him to collect it?

Thalina's plan died quickly with the guard's response to Acion.

"I am sorry, good visitor, but your credentials are incomplete. You will not be admitted to the palace, but you are welcome to leave any token intended for the king."

Those eyes narrowed. They were dark, filled with mystery. "It will be given to him?"

"It will be examined and, if deemed fitting, will be presented to the king."

Acion's voice hardened. "Deemed fitting by whom?"

Thalina smiled at his correct grammar, which enforced her theory that he might be an android.

"By his majesty's staff, of course."

"I calculate a forty-seven per cent chance that the gift will not actually be delivered. That is too high."

The sentry bristled. "Well, that depends upon what it is, doesn't it? No one will deliver anything to his majesty that might be deemed perilous..."

"Even words can be perilous," Acion declared, startling the guard to silence. "It is my instruction to deliver the gift to the king's own hand. If I cannot pass to do so, then I will depart."

"You will not pass."

Acion bowed. "Then I wish you good day." He pivoted and strode away, disappearing into the crowd. Thalina heard the sentry give a sigh of relief when Acion was out of sight.

She couldn't believe he'd give up on his assignment as

easily as that. He'd come from Cumae, which wasn't an easy journey. Cumae was one of the planets closest to Incendium but there was a meteor cluster between the two.

"Come, Thalina," her father said from behind her, clearly unaware of what she'd seen. "Let us leave the puzzle in capable hands."

Thalina rose and blocked the view of the screen she was watching from her father. The more detail kept from Ouros the better, especially when she was launching a scheme. "I would linger a little longer, Father. You know how the Vault fascinates me."

Ouros, perhaps predictably, wasn't fooled. He eyed his daughter and she feared he could read her thoughts. "The others call you trustworthy because you keep their secrets close," he rumbled. "But your mother and I both know that you keep your own secrets even closer." He raised a hand when she might have argued. "Do not be foolish, Thalina, and I will be content."

"Yes, Father. Thank you, Father."

Ouros had barely left the Vault when Thalina spun back to the display. The three guards were determined to resolve the issue of the lock as quickly as possible. One was dispatched by Ector to check the mechanism again. The second ran a diagnostic test and Ector himself began to tap instructions into a console.

No one was watching Thalina.

Acion wouldn't come back to the same gate, she reasoned. He wouldn't go to another obvious gate, either, because he'd assume that they were all centrally monitored. He might even know that for sure. He might try to enter the palace through a window, but that wouldn't be easily done either. Most of them were very high in the walls, higher than two men, for that very reason.

No, he'd use the river exit. She had to assume he had

a means to remove the grate or would find one. Thalina put the display of the sewer grate on the largest display.

She didn't have to wait long before a familiar figure came striding through the river water to the grill. The water was thigh-high for him and moving swiftly, but it presented no obstacle. She thrilled at the sight of his strength and purpose. He cut a direct path from the opposite bank to the grill. His gaze flicked upward, and Thalina guessed he had scheduled his emergence from the forest to coincide with the guards turning away. He was probably timing his progress.

His eyes glittered as he stepped into the shadow of the arch over the grill. Again, Thalina saw that his gaze was moving quickly as he gathered details. Too quickly. So, his vision was augmented like his left palm. What else? He surveyed the grill and its stone surround. She knew when he spotted the monitor because he seized it with his gloved hand. Thalina switched to the back-up feed to watch him pull the feed loose enough to disable it. An alarm might have rung but she overrode the system to ensure its silence.

It wouldn't have been easy to rip the feed from the mortar where it was embedded. His strength in that arm had to be augmented, as well.

Unless he was completely manufactured. The thrilling possibility made Thalina watch him even more intently.

Acion waited, then arched a brow that there wasn't an alarm. Thalina smiled as he waited a little longer, and guessed that he was calculating the best way to continue. He removed his left glove and flicked the end of his index finger with his thumb. The tip lifted, like a hinged lid, revealing a tiny hidden saw. Sparks flew as he cut the grill free from the rock around it. It must have been a powerful little saw, for it made quick work of the metal bars.

Thalina caught her breath at the sight of that

improvement. With each revelation, her conviction that he was an android increased.

"Wait," Ector said, but Thalina lifted a hand to silence him. She felt him and his companion come to stand behind her.

"I'll take care of it," she said with authority.

"But, princess..."

"He has a mission. I want to know what it is before he's stopped."

"But..."

"That is a command," Thalina said, interrupting the Captain of the Guard as firmly as her father might do. "You will not tell my father until my investigation is complete."

She was aware of their consternation but ignored it for the moment.

She was more interested in the way Acion bent half of the grill back, folding it against the other half as if it were more insubstantial than it was. Her companions gasped.

"That's impossible," said Ector.

"Not for him," she said softly, watching so intently that she didn't want to blink.

"Surely we should sound an alarm..."

"Surely you believe a dragon shifter can deter an intruder," Thalina said, rising to her feet.

"You shouldn't engage, princess. He might overpower you..."

"And I will fry him if he does."

The guards fell silent at that.

Thalina tapped up a map of the lowest level of the palace. She indicated the secured barriers to the Vault and tapped the screen to have more barriers lowered silently into place. "You can see that I've isolated him into this warren of passages. It will take him a bit of time to realize that all the ends are blinds and that there's no way to progress."

"But the Hoard is there," Ector protested.

"And more than adequately defended," Thalina argued. "This region is the best choice, given his location. If he moves beyond it, others could be endangered."

Ector's lips thinned. "And once he realized he's trapped? Look at his strength!"

"I'll confront him before then." Thalina indicated the largest chamber, which was an empty storeroom. "I will interrogate him here. You will listen for my command to secure the door once I have him inside, and will block all monitoring."

She turned to face them, seeing rebellion in their eyes. She stood tall and used her most commanding voice. "He won't surrender the secret of his mission easily. I suspect he may be an android."

"Then he'll be destroyed," Ector said.

"But first, we should determine why he is here," Thalina said. She spoke quickly, wanting to put her plan in motion before they thought of many objections. This would likely be her only opportunity to investigate such a creature, whether he was cyborg or android, and she wasn't going to miss it. "If I'm right, he'll prefer to self-destruct rather than betray his maker. The interrogation may be brutal, so there must be no evidence of it. Do you understand?"

They glanced at each other, then bowed in unison. "Yes, princess."

"You will secure the portals for one day and one night to allow for my interrogation. Then I will either deliver him or his remains to your custody."

Ector cleared his throat. "And what shall we tell your father if asked about your whereabouts, princess?"

"That I've gone to solve a riddle, of course." Thalina smiled, waited for their bow of agreement, then strode out of the Vault.

Fortunately, she'd dressed simply on this day. Acion might be convinced that she was just a serving maid. If he wasn't certain, he might account any discrepancies to local variation. Thalina found a basket on her way to the lower storerooms and, even better, an abandoned apron. She braided her hair and rubbed some dirt on her face and hands, securing doors behind herself as she hastened downward. She lit a candle before entering the secured warren where Acion had been contained.

The door sealed behind her, just as planned. She stifled a shiver, knowing she was locked into a small maze with this powerful intruder.

Was he an android? How much would she be able to investigate?

The air had become colder as she descended and Thalina could smell the river. She couldn't hear the activities of the palace any more, or the bustle of the town. There was only the silence of stone, and the faint sound of the flowing river. Her heart began to pound in anticipation of the challenge ahead.

That was before she approached the last corner, heard the stealthy step of the intruder, and smelled the Seed.

The Seed! The scent of it sent a surge through Thalina, one that weakened her knees with sexual desire and filled her very blood with longing. She leaned back against the wall, still out of sight, to recover from its assault. She then savored her body's reaction to that scent. It was just as she had been told. Powerful. Intoxicating. Wonderful.

There was no one else at this level of the palace, which meant that the intruder was the Carrier of her Seed.

Thalina closed her eyes to savor that. The revelation changed everything.

Acion's interrogation was going to be even more

interesting than she'd anticipated.

The prospect was enough to make her dizzy. Her every fantasy come true.

Thalina doubted Acion knew that he carried the Seed.

She wasn't even sure how it was possible, although its scent made it difficult for her to reason clearly. She supposed an android could only be a receptacle for the seed, or a delivery mechanism, while a cyborg could be a true Carrier of the Seed, depending upon the specifics of his nature. Could either be her HeartKeeper? Not an android, certainly. A cyborg? It would depend on what parts of him had been replaced.

That just gave her more to investigate and explore. Thalina would have a gift from Acion before he left Incendium, in addition to relieving him of whatever token he had brought the king.

Acion heard the woman before he saw her. There was a bend in the passageway ahead of him and she was around the corner but out of his view. A light shone around the corner, and it flickered, leading him to the conclusion that she carried a candle. By the sound of the step, he assessed the probability of her gender and affirmed his theory by her scent.

Young. Mortal. Female.

Aroused.

That detail was definitely against the probabilities. Perhaps she liked the darkness. Perhaps she came to meet a lover secretly. Acion found this probable until he discerned that there were no other persons within the vicinity.

She was perhaps twenty paces away.

She was alone, in the lowest level of the palace. He smelled dirt on her skin, as well as a trace of perspiration. She sighed audibly and put something down. It didn't sound heavy.

A servant? That was the most likely scenario.

Acion eased closer and peeked around the corner. She was pretty and slender, with fair skin and brown hair pulled back in a braid. She sighed as if tired and looked about herself with a futility that Acion associated with those compelled to perform menial tasks. Her basket was empty and he calculated the probability to be very high— eighty-six per cent—that these rooms were used for storage.

If she'd been sent to fetch something, why was she aroused? The juxtaposition couldn't be resolved to Acion's satisfaction so he attributed the detail to some irrational quirk in her nature. Perhaps she found cellars exciting. Desire was often irrational in his experience.

The important detail was that she would have free rein to at least part of the palace and a knowledge of its design.

He would take advantage of the opportunity presented. She would be his assistant, willing or not.

She turned her back upon him, as unaware of his presence as he expected, and opened a door. Her candle didn't cast much light within the room, which meant it might be large. She bent to pick up the basket before entering the room and Acion took advantage of her inattention.

He moved like a flash of lightning, grabbing her and locking a hand over her mouth. She made a little cry of surprise and dropped both candle and basket. The candle rolled on the ground and Acion stepped on it, extinguishing the flame. She fought him, so Acion carried her into the storeroom, pinning her against the wall as he kicked the door closed, sealing them in darkness.

She was slender but sweetly curved, and his body responded to having her in his embrace. Acion frowned, because the complication of a physical reaction at this time was unnecessary, unprecedented, and illogical.

His mission was of greatest importance.

"You will help me reach the king," he whispered into her ear. "Or I will break your neck. The chance of you dying after sustaining such an injury is high, but it increases to one hundred per cent if I abandon you and you aren't found. I *will* abandon you, and I will ensure you aren't found. Do you understand?"

She caught her breath, then nodded. The sign of her vulnerability made him want to recant his threat, which made no sense.

Acion knew he sounded more stern when he continued. "And you will not reveal me. Do you understand?"

She nodded again.

There was a risk that she might trick him, but Acion calculated it to be so small as to be irrelevant. She was at a serious disadvantage. They were alone and he was both larger and stronger than her. He did not find it likely that anyone would hear her, even if she screamed, he could not sense the presence of another person, and he could certainly fulfill his threat to her and be prepared for an assault before it could arrive. If she *was* meeting a lover and that individual wasn't nearby, that person had to arrive, to find her and to battle Acion, which surely was a losing proposition.

The situation was almost ideal.

So, Acion released the serving maid—which is what she had to be—only to discover that his calculations had omitted one very important variable.

CHAPTER TWO

The maid didn't scream or surrender meekly.
She fought.
And she fought well.

In fact, she battled Acion with a strength disproportionate to her size.

Acion took a strike to the face before he could evade her quick fist. He grabbed at her, but she ducked, spinning into the darkened chamber like a whirlwind. She was either bold or foolish to move in such darkness! Or perhaps she was familiar with the room's contents. He tapped his right temple, turning on the light embedded in his brow, and something quickened within him at the sight of her.

She was crouched, her eyes glittering, her hands raised. Her hair was coming loose from her braid, as if it moved of its own volition. If he'd been more fanciful than it was possible for an android to be, he might have seen flames light in her eyes. But that was impossible, so he knew it had to be a trick.

The chamber, to his surprise, was empty. Why had she entered it? Acion could find no reasonable explanation.

Even as he considered this, he moved swiftly, striking three blows in rapid succession, but pulling back slightly before connecting with her. He needed to capture her, not injure or incapacitate her. She was no good to him dead. She was smaller than him, female, and undoubtedly more fragile, yet blocked his blows with unexpected ease. In fact, she attacked him, with no regard for ensuring that he wasn't injured. He defended himself, a little less easily than might have been ideal, and recognized that he was hampered by his need to avoid hurting her.

She took advantage of his choice, kicking him hard in the gut, then striking at his brow so hard with the heel of her hand that the light was smashed. Acion stumbled backward, amazed that she could hit with such power.

She struck like a warrior, as well, not slapping or scratching as women without military training often did. Her moves were decisive and clean, so forceful that it took him a moment to realize that she meant to disable but not kill him. Acion took a kick to the gut and dropped to one knee, assessing.

She was absurdly fast.

The conclusion was inevitable: she was an android, as well.

His processors spun, drawing data from his brief and comparing it with the furious fighting skills of the woman. There were officially no androids on Incendium, which was an odd detail, but that didn't mean there weren't any secretly on the planet.

Like himself.

If there were androids being developed and trained secretly, learning more about her would provide useful information to the Hive.

If there were androids infiltrating Incendium society for some other purpose, learning more about this one would provide useful information to the Hive.

Acion existed to serve.

He immediately decided to let her win. She wanted to subdue him, which meant she had a plan—and learning the details of that plan would tell Acion a great deal about her programming. She lunged at him, driving two fingers hard into his throat, a point of vulnerability for men, and he was assured that she didn't know the truth of his nature.

Acion fell, as a man would.

How would she explain the broken light in his brow? Would she conclude he was a cyborg? That seemed probable, especially when he took the blow like a man.

Acion made it look as if he hit his head on the floor and let his body go limp. He turned on all of his sensors, determined to gather as much data as he could.

She leaned over him, still poised to fight. She had a light as well, because Acion saw its illumination through his eyelids but he didn't open his eyes to look. She surveyed him. She checked that he was breathing.

Then, to his astonishment, she touched her lips to his, a gesture of intimacy that sent a strange fire through his body.

"Mine," she whispered, her claim giving him a strange thrill. She then seized his ankle and dragged him from the chamber back into the corridor, once again showing that remarkable strength.

Where was she taking him? What would she do with him once they reached their destination? Would she take him closer to the royal chambers? Would she present him as a prize to the king? Or was she a spy of some kind?

Why claim him as her own? That and her kiss hinted at a more private conquest, although there was no telling what sexual practices were common on Incendium. Those details were lacking from his brief, much to Acion's annoyance. He found incomplete information caused unnecessary inefficiencies and it was unlike the Hive to be sloppy.

The details must not be known.

Or not available to him at this time.

The woman dragged him, her ability to do so despite

his considerable weight only buttressing to the probability of his conclusion. Acion tabulated to the best of his abilities, but her destination, once he recognized what it was, astonished him all the same.

"The princess has abandoned her own plan," Ector said to his subordinate, Salvon, knowing his concern was clear.

"Women can be impulsive," Salvon replied. They watched the security display together, their uncertainty palpable. "She *did* command that we not tell the king of her activities."

"But her welfare is our responsibility. Why would she change the plan?"

Salvon caught his breath as the princess flung down her prize at the end of the corridor. She approached the barred door there with its glowing lock and raised one hand.

The Hoard.

"She wouldn't," whispered Salvon in horror. Princess Thalina gave the command and the door to the Hoard slid open. Both men winced.

"She is," corrected Ector. "I must tell the king."

The Seed had a power that Thalina hadn't anticipated. Its scent awakened her senses, fed her desire, and made it impossible to think of anything other than mating with Acion. It awakened a desire to possess that was so primal and overwhelming that Thalina was shocked. It gave her a strength beyond her usual abilities, as well, and a sense of invincibility.

There was no question of denying its demand.

She'd known that Acion's reaction would be quick, and she had hoped that hers was quicker. Against a non-shifting mortal, she knew she'd be faster—against a cyborg or android, she wasn't sure. The uncertainty had added a little more spice to their first fight.

But he had let her win. Thalina was curious about that choice, but glad of it. She didn't want to shift shape in his presence, not yet. She didn't want to reveal all of her secrets.

Not until she had the Seed.

The Seed changed her plan, too. She wouldn't claim him in a dirty storage room in the bowels of the palace. That deed deserved dignity and honor. Cleanliness and comfort. She didn't dare take him to her chambers without knowing what threat he posed to her father or family, if any. There was only one place close enough that would suffice. She hauled his weight to the entry to her father's treasury, commanded the portal to open, and smiled as the armored interior was revealed.

The Hoard was a fortress. The walls were of the strongest metal known to their kind. The doors couldn't be forced open, and the chamber could be defended from within. The treasury had been built as a safe room and sanctuary, a last place to defend in the case of the worst siege. It dated from the era of Scintillon himself and was the oldest part of the palace, though it had been buttressed as the palace had been built around it.

No one would be able to interfere.

And Acion wouldn't be able to escape.

Thalina dragged him into the Hoard, knowing that she would be pursued and soon. The guards would be too late, though. She was in. She laid her hand upon the panel beside the door for her print to be scanned.

"Secure portal," she commanded and the doors closed. A sequence of hidden latches clicked in rapid succession.

They were safe, at least until Ouros commanded the portal to open. There was no door in Incendium that could be barred against the king.

She should be quick.

"Illuminate," Thalina commanded and torches sprang to light around the perimeter of the room. They were mounted in the walls, well above Thalina's head in her human form, and powered by a crystal generator buried beneath the floor. The lights and the generator itself warmed the floor, taking the chill of stone from the refuge.

The chamber of the Hoard was round and of considerable size, built to accommodate the dimensions of the royal family in their dragon forms. No earlier King of Incendium had had as many children as Ouros, and Thalina had to admit that it would be a bit cramped for her and her eleven sisters as well as their parents to take refuge in the Hoard, if they had all assumed their dragon forms.

The Hoard held the sum of Ouros' treasury, gold and gems and jewels inventoried and stacked behind numbered panels in the walls. Most believed that the wealth of the Hoard was in those material treasures, but Thalina knew better. The more important panels secured information and records.

In the middle of the chamber was a fountain that splashed, providing clean water and a welcome noise, one that disguised the truth of the occupants being essentially buried alive. To one side were stores of foodstuffs, preserved and compressed to provide sufficient nourishment to the family and their retainers for the duration of a long siege. There were couches and tables, games and pastimes, as well as monitors of the world beyond the Hoard. Those monitors were currently dark, and Thalina intended to keep them that way.

"Full defensive mode," Thalina commanded as she tugged Acion to a couch beside the fountain. Plates of metal slid into place over the door, securing them inside, and she felt his interest.

She was glad he was awake.

She then strode to the bank of displays. "Kill monitors and key release to a single word in my voice," she said, turning slightly to watch Acion. "The command that secures Princess Callida's diary will be the word."

Acion's eyes flicked. Thalina knew he was searching his databanks for references, but he wouldn't find that one.

Callida didn't think anyone knew it, and it was only an accident that Thalina did. Her sister would have to be added to the security loop to approve the release, but that was incidental. Thalina needed a word that Acion couldn't possibly know or figure out.

Callida might not be overly inclined to reveal her code word to the security forces of the palace—she'd have to vent frustration with Thalina over the violation of privacy first—but Thalina didn't intend to use the release word soon.

It could take a long time to ensure that she had the Seed.

She wanted at least the day and night that she'd ordered, and wondered if her father would allow it.

She had best begin the seduction soon, not that the scent of the Seed allowed any other possibilities to enter her thoughts. She licked her lips without meaning to do as much, and knew that Acion noted the gesture.

"This is not the agreed protocol," came a voice.

"I've changed it due to an unexpected development."

There was a pause. "Of course, princess," Ector ceded, and she was sure he'd already sent word to her father.

Thalina watched Acion scan the room through narrowed eyes, his gaze lingering for the merest instant on three points. She'd bet that was where the speakers were hidden. "We will secure Princess Callida's assistance in this matter. Portal sealed. Oxygen feeding. Monitors off in three...two...one."

There was an audible click and then silence.

"I know you're awake," Thalina said. "And I know you let me win. Will you tell me why?"

Acion opened his eyes. He sat up and openly surveyed the room, then surveyed her.

Assessed her.

Thalina could almost hear his processors sorting and discarding courses of action.

"This is the Hoard," he said, no question in his voice.

"It is."

"Why would you bring an intruder to the treasury of Incendium?"

"Because it's the one place we can't be easily interrupted."

Their gazes locked and held for a long moment, and she was interested that he didn't ask the obvious question. Instead he stood, then walked toward her with steady steps. Thalina didn't move, but she thrilled at the scent of the Seed drawing near. Her heart was thundering and she wondered if he knew it.

Acion stopped right in front of her, looking and undoubtedly gathering her biometrics. "You are not what you appear to be," he said, without inflection. "It is unlikely that a serving maid would have such authority, although she might know that secret word."

"And you're not what you appear to be," she countered. It was fascinating to watch him gather information and choose his reaction. He was a much more sophisticated device than any of the automatons she'd taken apart to study.

Acion regarded her, his head slightly tilted. It was a good imitation of curiosity, so good that she wondered if he could be curious. "I do not understand your meaning." He gestured to himself. "I am precisely as I appear to be." His voice warmed, as if he sought to gain her trust, and Thalina wasn't fooled.

She braced herself for his move. The scent of the Seed sent a confusing heat through her body and she hoped it didn't slow her reactions too much.

It did. Acion abruptly closed the distance and seized her tightly before she could evade him. His arms locked around her again, and Thalina felt her body respond to his touch once more, long enough that he caught her by surprise.

It took a moment for Thalina to realize that he held a knife at her throat. Interestingly, it was an actual weapon, a knife from his belt, not a device hidden within his fingertips.

"You will aid my escape from this chamber and ensure my access to the palace, whoever you are," he growled into her ear. "Use the release word."

Thalina laughed. "I won't." She felt the tip of the knife move against her throat. She rubbed herself against him a little and was glad to feel his body's reaction. Her new confidence was clear in her tone. "The odds of you injuring me without being certain of my identity is very low, perhaps one in three."

He paused for just an instant, considering that.

Thalina twisted in his grip in that moment, wanting to watch his eyes as he worked through the ramifications.

"You are very sure," he said softly, his face very close to hers.

"Completely sure," Thalina agreed in a whisper. "Because I know that you're not a thief, breaking into the palace, which is what I'd expect of someone who forced entry through a neglected portal. You're certainly not desperate or cornered, and you won't make such a foolish decision as to hurt the one person, maybe the only person, who could help you complete your mission."

His gaze flicked. "My mission?"

"To deliver a gift to the king."

"There is a second security feed," he concluded, no

doubt in his tone.

"Of course. Dragons don't like being surprised."

It was a hint but one he didn't take. Thalina wondered if his ability to adapt to new information was being overwhelmed. She doubted it. There must be more variables to consider than she'd realized. "But how could you know my mission?"

"If I saw one security feed, what are the probabilities I would have seen another?"

His eyes narrowed. "Ninety-six per cent." His lips tightened. "The probability that a serving maid would have seen either is negligible. Who are you?"

"Why would I surrender my one advantage so quickly?"

"You would not," he murmured. His grip upon her had loosened slightly.

Thalina pushed the blade of his knife aside with a fingertip. "I think we should negotiate," she said, running a hand over his shoulder. "Are you a cyborg or an android?"

He put a little distance between them, but didn't lower the knife even as he regarded her with new wariness. He certainly didn't answer her question. "Are you one of the fabled sirens of Incendium's marketplace?"

"No, although I'm intrigued that you would ask." Thalina said and stretched to touch her lips to his throat. She could feel his pulse there and the warmth of his skin. "It seems we have a certain urge in common." No matter whether he was augmented or fully android, intimacy might be the best way to investigate his abilities. "Let's make a deal, Acion," she whispered into his ear.

His gaze swept over her again, then lingered on her mouth. "I see no cause to bargain."

"No? Even though the door is sealed forever, without my release command?"

"I could compel you to give it."

Thalina shook her head. "You won't."

"All beings can be persuaded to part with information."

"Not this one."

Their gazes locked again. She liked to watch the automatons work, but this was infinitely better. Was there a way she could see the workings that led him to make decisions? "You are not in a position to barter."

"Neither are you." Thalina decided to provoke him with a guess. "Unless it's your goal to rust away in the darkness here, sealed forever in a chamber designed to provide shelter for years."

"Rust," he echoed, tilting his head again. "A whimsical choice of word."

"Rust," Thalina repeated. She touched his finger, the one with the hinged tip that concealed a tiny saw. "A perfectly apt choice of word for an android." She kissed him below the jaw and saw his throat work. "But you're not just any android, are you, Acion?"

He spun away from her touch then, retreating to pace. He took a deep breath and glared at her when he reached the couch beside the fountain. "You are neither serving maid nor whore. You are not a guard in the king's service. Who are you and what do you desire of me?"

"I want the truth, first of all," Thalina replied. "Tell me why you came to the palace."

"That information is not available to you at this time."

"What gift did you bring the king?"

"That information is not available to anyone at this time."

"Show it to me, then."

He straightened and folded his arms across his chest, looking both formidable and resolute. No machine could appear so enticing. He must be a cyborg. "That request does not cohere with the instructions in my assignment."

Thalina took slow steps toward him, as if she stalked him. She supposed she was stalking him. She liked how avidly he watched her and deliberately took a deep breath, savoring the scent of the Seed. His eyes brightened and she knew he noticed her body's reaction.

"Who sent you?" she asked.

"That information is not available to you at this time."

She stopped in front of him, folding her arms across her chest. She saw him glance down at her cleavage, then swallow. "But here's what I really want to know," she whispered. "How can you be the Carrier of the Seed?"

She'd shocked him. Thalina saw that immediately. He frowned and looked down at her in confusion, then his eyes revealed that he was reviewing the information he had about Incendium. "The Carrier of the Seed is the man who can impregnate one of the royal dragon shifter princesses of Incendium," he said, as if reciting from a reference source. Thalina supposed that was exactly what he was doing. "This cannot be the case. You are testing my knowledge of Incendium in an attempt to put me at a disadvantage..."

Thalina closed her hand over his erection and he inhaled sharply before he stopped speaking. He was scanning her, seeking the solution to the mystery in her eyes. He was hard in her grip, hard enough that she tingled in anticipation of claiming him. He took a slow breath and she knew he was assessing the magnitude of her arousal.

"You are the Carrier of the Seed," she murmured. "Your sensors are providing evidence of my response to that truth."

His voice dropped to a hoarse whisper. "But that means that you are one of the dragon shifter princesses of Incendium."

Thalina smiled. "It does. It also means that you must be a cyborg, not an android."

His gaze flicked.

Thalina was intrigued. "An android couldn't be the Carrier of the Seed."

Acion ignored her comment. "It is my understanding that dragon shifters cannot deny the opportunity to accept the Seed."

"That is correct."

He nodded slightly, apparently reassured. "So, the wager you would logically propose would be my surrender of the Seed in exchange for my freedom from the Hoard."

"That would be an excellent start." Thalina couldn't resist the urge to tease him a little. "What would you calculate to be the probability of a successful exchange?"

"In excess of ninety-eight per cent," he said immediately. "With some allowance for slight variations in our physical compatibility, coupling abilities, and sexual customs in our respective cultures." Thalina knew her surprise at his precision showed. "I have the necessary programming and physical enhancements for sexual functionality and performed in the top percentile of my class in assessment."

"What benchmarks were used in the assessment?" Thalina asked before she could stop herself.

Acion counted them on his fingers. "Physical dimensions, endurance, technique, variation in technique, adaptability to a partner's needs, and successful simulation of foreplay." He nodded. "That was calculated based on the partner's biometric response."

"And how would you calculate mine right now?"

He studied her with a little frown, then cupped her chin to look into her eyes. "Your pupils are dilated, a sign of arousal in humanoids. I can smell that your labia are wet, an indication of your preparedness for union. Your pulse has accelerated steadily since our enclosure in this room, and your breathing rate has also increased since we have touched each other. Your skin is warm and flushed, a sign of heightened circulation." He ran a hand over her breast. "And the erectile tissue in your nipples is contracted. I would calculate your arousal to be between seven and eight on a scale of ten, with seventy per cent surety."

"Why the seventy per cent?" Thalina asked, hearing that her words were breathless. His touch was sending fire through her veins, undoubtedly because of the vehement call of the Seed.

"I have no data upon the signs of sexual arousal in dragon shifters and am thus assuming that while in the humanoid form, a dragon shifter exhibits similar signs to those found in humans who are not dragon shifters. This is by no means a certainty, though, and my conclusion must be qualified."

"Your assumption is correct."

His brows rose in relief. "Then your arousal must be between seven and eight on a scale of ten." He pursed his lips, clearly confronted by a question.

"What is it?"

"I must consider whether desire is increased in dragon shifters in the same way as in non-shifting humans."

"It is."

He was calculating again, but now there was a small smile curving his lips. "Then I must increase the probability of a successful union."

"And what about your arousal?" Thalina caressed him.

"My arousal remains steady at five on the same scale, an optimal level to provide satisfaction without incurring any unnecessarily impairment of my awareness or responsiveness."

Maybe it was the dragon in Thalina, but that confession made her determined to push Acion's arousal rate past ten on that particular chart.

"Only five?" she purred and he nodded. "Let me see what I can do about that."

Acion was intrigued. Not only were there secret androids on Incendium, but this one insisted that she was one of the royal family.

The notion was ridiculous. No princess would be permitted to challenge an intruder without protection. Perhaps he was to provide a test of her functionality. It was remarkable to consider that they might have similar assignments, but when he considered how often androids tested enhancements to their functionality, the prospect was clearly likely.

Perhaps there was a plan to replace the legendary sirens of their market with androids. Such a scheme would undoubtedly improve efficiency in servicing clients seeking sexual pleasure and Acion knew it would diminish biological contamination.

This was a possibility that made sense, more sense than her assertion that he was the Carrier of the Seed. He wasn't a cyborg, and so there couldn't be a biological facet to his nature, such as would be the case if he were the Carrier of the Seed. No, he'd been trapped for a purpose. She'd been determined to capture him but not injure him, so as to avoid damaging his reactions in any way.

He must be her test.

He should mate with her, as she said she desired, and look for verifying signs of her true nature. An android, of course, would not be able to shift shape and become a dragon. This could explain why she hadn't done as much already.

Acion had never mated with an android himself,

though he had been used to grant pleasure to various mortal Warrior Maidens of Cumae. This android presented him with yet another opportunity to serve by gathering information.

She was attractive and stimulated his reaction, although he had to admit that much of her appeal was her intelligence. She analyzed in a way that he understood perfectly. She was fearless, as he had been programmed to be. They might have been two sides of the same coin.

He supposed that they were.

A feigned role as one of the dragon shifter princesses would explain her access to the security information. Had she been made to resemble Callida? That was the only princess she had named, and might explain her knowledge of Callida's secret code. Acion launched a subroutine to pull the images of all twelve dragon princesses and compare their features to those of this woman.

Thalina. The conclusion was reached by his facial recognition programming and he verified the result. She certainly resembled the third daughter of King Ouros and Queen Ignita. He would have to continue his investigation to decide why such a course of action had been pursued.

Acion did all of this reasoning by the time Thalina caught his face in her hands, rose to her toes, and touched her lips to his. Acion anticipated a sweet kiss, a gentle beginning to a temperate coupling, but she surprised him. The first touch of her lips was beguiling and left him hungry for more. As soon as he leaned down and caught her around the waist, lifting her against him, her mouth locked over his with unexpected demand. She backed him into the couch, and he stumbled, then fell back upon it. She tumbled atop him, no doubt by design, without breaking her incendiary kiss.

Acion closed his eyes, knowing he had never been

kissed with such fervor. He concluded that there was no
need to be as gentle as he usually was, not when his
partner was as strong as he and unlikely to be injured. He
tried to respond in kind to ensure that the test of her
abilities was thorough, his need to serve overwhelming all
other impulses. She moaned into his mouth and straddled
him, the scent of her need feeding his own arousal.

He knew he should have been making observations
about the caliber of her programming, the sophistication
of her form, the simulation of biological surfaces and
reactions. But her tongue was between his teeth, her
fingers locked around his head, her breasts crushed
against his chest. She kissed him with a savage passion
that almost ignited his circuits and certainly drove all
calculation from his thoughts. Acion felt as if a fire swept
through him, frying all logic and leaving him hungry for
more sensation. She wound one leg around his and
rubbed her belly against his erection, prompting a
reaction that was quicker than any he'd experienced
before.

"Kiss me back, Acion," she growled against his
throat, even though he was already doing so. The raw
need in her voice sent sparks through him. He caught her
buttocks in his hands and rolled on top of her, deepening
their kiss and pinning her down. He felt a curious sense
of satisfaction when she purred with pleasure and grazed
his mouth with the edge of her teeth. She ripped open his
shirt in her impatience and her hands roved over his skin.
The way she touched him was proprietary, as if he was a
pleasure slave commanded to serve her, and Acion
extrapolated her desire from that.

He kissed her ear, her neck, the hollow of her throat,
the ripe perfection of her breast. He lifted her skirts and
slid down the length of her to lick her wet sex. She
gasped, surprised in her turn, then parted her legs as his
mouth closed over her. The attention to detail in her

sexual organs was a clear sign to Acion that he had guessed her intended purpose correctly, for he'd never seen an android that so perfectly replicated a woman, in both shape, design, and function. She was gloriously wet and her labia engorged, her clitoris perfectly sensitive.

Acion feasted upon her, holding her hips so that she was captive to his intimate kiss, and monitored her arousal. It was easily nine on that scale of ten when she sat up and seized him, rolling him to his back again as she tore open his chausses. Her hand was locked around him, her hair wild and her cheeks flushed.

He was astonished to note that his own arousal was in excess of seven.

And that was before she climbed atop him like a warrior queen, claiming him and drawing him deep inside her warmth. He faltered for a moment, shaken by the unprecedented wave of pleasure that rolled through him, then she moved her hips, demanding more. She rode him, holding him captive between her thighs and watching as she insisted upon more and more. She tore off her own chemise, giving him a view of her fine breasts, and he couldn't resist the temptation. He reached up, cupping one in each palm, teasing the taut nipples with his thumbs, and was proud of her obvious pleasure. She arched her back and moved with greater speed, her slick heat drawing him deeper within her. Acion found his heart racing, his breath coming quickly, his erection harder than it had even been before.

"Still five?" she asked, then bent and kissed his ear. Her tongue rolled in his ear and he closed his eyes, dizzy at the tumult she awakened in him.

"Almost eight," he admitted.

She clicked her tongue. "The claiming of the Seed merits at least a ten," she chided and he saw the challenge in her eyes.

He assessed her response. "You are almost at ten."

She gave him a wicked smile. "I don't want to be there alone."

Of course, pleasure should be reciprocal to ensure that clients returned for more.

Even so, Acion wasn't certain his systems could tolerate a higher reading than he was currently experiencing. His reasoning processes were compromised. He couldn't think of anything except the woman atop him and the pleasure she was giving him. He was hot. He was agitated. His processes were consumed with combinations and permutations of sexual activity, and an almost frantic need to deduce which would grant this siren the most pleasure.

He reached between them and found the hard bud of her clitoris. He touched it gently with his fingertip, heard her gasp in delight, then knew.

He withdrew his hand enough to remove the tip of his middle finger and launch the small motor. He felt its hum more than he heard it, then pressed the soft vibrating tip, the one that was usually hidden away, against her clitoris.

She gasped and her eyes flew open. She stared at him as the color left her cheeks.

Acion held her gaze, increased the speed slightly and rubbed that vibrating fingertip against her. She moaned, a sound of such capitulation that he felt a primitive pride in his choice.

Then he pinched the clitoris between the vibrating fingertip and his plain index fingertip.

His partner roared. She bucked. She drew him deep inside her by some skill he'd not confronted before, then locked her legs around him. He was captive, snared inside her, barely able to move, as she convulsed and bellowed in her release.

And in the sight of her pleasure, at the mercy of her sensory demand, Acion wanted only more. He caught her around the waist, rolled her to her back and thrust even deeper Heat surged within him, fusing their desires, making the experience of her pleasure as powerful as his own. He was certain that his desire reached a ten, if not exceeding that point on the scale, but he couldn't stop. He managed two more strokes before the fire raced through him, his mind went blank, and the Seed—if indeed he carried it—was surrendered in an explosive rush.

Then he laid his temple on the couch as his body rhythms returned to normal. It took so much longer than usual that he wondered what had just happened to him. He felt seared, cauterized on the inside…and lighter. Sexual intimacy had never been so extreme an experience for him, and Acion knew there had to be a reason why it had been different this time.

But for the moment, he was too exhausted to consider the riddle.

And that was just as strange.

He needed to recharge and restore. He launched his own rejuvenation sequences without opening his eyes, knowing the nanobots in his system would seek out all places in need of repair.

What was happening to him on Incendium?

Was he changing?

Was it because of his new programming?

Or was it because of this android and some unprecedented abilities she possessed?

Who *was* her maker?

Acion had insufficient information to make a satisfactory conclusion. His heart skipped with what might have been trepidation—if he had possessed the programming to experience such a sensation.

He had time to realize that the probability of his now having such abilities might be higher than previously before the rejuvenation system slowed his thoughts.

Acion was put into a resting state similar to the one humans called sleep, his calculations stilled for the moment.

CHAPTER THREE

It was clear to Thalina that she needed a cyborg of her own, one that she'd use just to ensure her sexual pleasure. That finger was a wonderful augmentation and one that should be given to all men. Maybe Thalina would request it for all of her future lovers. She'd never had a mating as powerful as this one and was sure the next time would be better. It was clear that Acion's intellectual capacities were also augmented, which would make him a learning machine.

Next time, he'd send her over Incendium's moon.

He might just be the perfect companion. She wondered if he would be able to perform sexually at more frequent intervals than a man. Thalina had found her previous partners a bit disappointing in that regard.

As a dragon, she had appetites, after all.

It seemed highly probable that she could expect improved performance. She smiled, hearing the influence of Acion's way of expressing himself on her own speech. She liked how he talked and how he reasoned everything through. She liked talking to him, and listening to him.

One day and night wasn't going to be nearly enough.

She remained stretched out beside Acion as he appeared to doze, amused that he would have a similar reaction to a human after sexual release. It was comfortably warm in the Hoard and the sound of the fountain was soothing. Thalina felt as if she had stolen a day out of time, and already she didn't want it to end. The scent of the Seed was reassuring in an odd way, now that she'd claimed it once.

Would they have the chance to do it again?

Reminded of the passing time, Thalina sat up and surveyed Acion. She might not have another chance to investigate him. He was nude beside her and looked like a man in almost every way. He had very little body hair, which was a good thing to Thalina's thinking, just a little dark patch in the middle of his chest. He was extremely well muscled, as if he exercised rigorously, and she wondered if he had to do that, or it this was just the way he was made. His skin looked to be tanned, but she realized on closer examination that it was the same hue everywhere.

As if he sunbathed nude.

Maybe he did.

She couldn't discern any seams or joins in his body, which she supposed said a great deal for the quality of the membrane that encased him. It even felt warm and was flexible, like skin. She caressed his hip, wanting to feel him again, and thought she might wake him up. He didn't stir at all, so she explored more boldly.

His face was smooth, as if he had just shaved, and she wondered whether he even grew whiskers. There was a line on his forehead, over his right eye, like a scar. She knew that was where the broken light had been located. His head was smooth, too, as if it was shaved, but Thalina considered that might be simpler than planting hair follicles. The only ornament he wore was the silver ring on his right thumb, and she peered at it, trying to discern the pattern. It looked like a band of entwined lines, but she couldn't make sense of it. A blue tattoo peeked out from beneath it, maybe a more permanent mark with a similar meaning. Embedded in his left palm was that thin computer, much like the one she wore on the inside of her left forearm, but fixed in place and smaller.

She wondered whether she could explore that computer's contents without disturbing him and glanced back at his face.

The line on his forehead was gone.

Thalina leaned over Acion, focusing her gaze on that spot. The skin—or membrane—was repaired and seamlessly so, as if there had never been an injury.

He wasn't sleeping. He was undergoing repair.

He didn't seem to be breathing, at least not deeply, and was very still. Thalina leaned over him and felt the barest whisper of breath emanating from his nostrils. She placed a hand on his chest and felt that his heartbeat had slowed considerably, much more than to a resting rate for a biological organism. She had to wait for each successive beat.

All of his energy was being put into repair.

She surveyed him, impressed and amazed, and wanting to know more. Digits lit on the computer screen in his palm, and steadily counted down from one hundred. Thalina was pretty sure he'd wake up when the count reached zero, his systems restored to their previous capacity.

Fascinating.

The digital numbers reached single digits as she wondered, then his computer emitted a faint beep as the one change to a zero.

Acion's eyes opened and he sat up. Thalina heard his pulse increase rapidly, then settle at a steady but increased rate. He surveyed her, then rose from the couch to dress. When he turned, tugging on his chausses, Thalina smiled at the evidence of her theory being true. "Back to five?" she asked.

Acion nodded. "It is an excellent resting status."

"Why not three?"

He pursed his lips, and she wondered whether he was seeking the answer or deciding how much of it to tell her. "Most warriors fight better when emotionally engaged in the result. Even non-warriors fight better when they believe their own survival to be at risk. This is called the fight-or-flight-response."

Thalina tugged on her skirt and chemise. "Fear stimulates a hormonal reaction that gives the organism greater strength and agility in the short term."

Acion nodded. "But my survival is seldom at risk, since most foes are inferior." He spoke with such conviction that Thalina smiled. "And maybe the survival of the individual doesn't matter that much in the end."

"How so?"

"A biological organism exists in isolation, in most cases. Its memories and experiences belong to itself alone, and its sense of identity is strong as a result. An android is linked to a server and shares all experiences, as you know, so is really more like a single cell in the collective mind."

As she knew? How would she know that?

And why was he calling himself an android? Wasn't he a cyborg?

Thalina didn't want to interrupt him to ask. It seemed like a smarter choice to listen.

"Technically, the fight-or-flight response means that the brain, upon perceiving a threat, stimulates the hypothalamus to secrete the hormones cortisol and adrenaline into the bloodstream of the organism." Acion's words flowed smoothly as he tugged on his boots. He didn't seem to care that his boots and chausses, and even the hem of his cloak, were still wet from the river. "This results in a number of physical reactions, including an increased heart and breathing rate, and a tighter focus of attention and loss of peripheral vision. Other signs are diluted pupils, bladder relaxation, flushed skin and shaking, as well as slowed digestive processes."

"But these reactions are triggered by the perception of a threat."

"Exactly, which means that the fight-or-flight response is always less vigorous in androids, even those who have the necessary stimulants—or equivalents—in their systems, because androids do not perceive threats as readily as biological organisms."

"And how does this tie back to an arousal rate of five?"

Acion lifted a finger. "The Hive, in its brilliance, engineered this approximation of the extra level of power. Testosterone, while a steroid, is strongly linked with competitiveness, as well as aggression and violence. It has proven to be a more reliable trigger in highly advanced androids than adrenaline or cortisol, and one that provides a similar burst of energy and desire to triumph."

"How clever. And a five?"

"Has been determined through extensive testing to be the optimal resting point, in order to allow for a response of acceptable timing."

"To approximate that of the fight-or-flight response?"

Acion nodded, then looked around the chamber, as if seeking a means of escape. He still appeared to be slightly aroused, and Thalina liked that this was his resting state.

She was more than ready to encourage his reaction.

Maybe even time it.

She was fascinated by the information he'd shared and wanted to know more. An android! If that was true, he was more highly developed than she could have imagined. Thalina wanted to know more.

The Hive must be where he'd been created. "Tell me

about the Hive."

Acion's expression changed immediately, and she knew she'd asked too much.

"That information is not available to you at this time." He straightened his garments and stood before her, then bowed. "I have fulfilled my half of the wager. I would request that you now release me from this chamber so that I can complete my mission."

"I'm not sure that the Seed has been properly surrendered," Thalina said. "There is a conviction amongst the dragon shifters of Incendium that the Seed must be delivered multiple times to ensure a satisfactory result." She watched his eyes flick as he assessed this.

"That information is not included in my brief."

"Perhaps it wasn't made available to you, because it wasn't foreseen that you would have need of it." Thalina smiled when he met her gaze. "It is quite improbable that you would be the Carrier of the Seed. Providing additional detail would simply have wasted memory."

He nodded immediately. "That is logical. I would request a second item from you then, in exchange for a second delivery of the Seed."

"A second bargain." Thalina nodded, watching him all the while. What would he ask for? "Such as?"

Acion didn't speak immediately. He cleared his throat, and Thalina was intrigued. It seemed almost as if he was shy.

Shy?

Impossible. He was a machine!

Still, Acion dropped his gaze from hers and cleared his throat again. "I would appreciate the opportunity to see a dragon while I am on Incendium, if it can be arranged."

Thalina considered him, wondering at this request. It seemed very un-android-like.

But his lovemaking had been, as well.

She realized in that moment just how low her expectation of androids had been. They weren't as easily identified as she'd anticipated. They weren't like automatons in the least.

They were much more interesting—or at least this one was.

That was when she saw the flaw in his logic, revealed by his request. "But I told you that you were the Carrier of the Seed."

Acion shook his head. "A highly improbable situation. I thought it might be impolite to challenge you at the time, but your conclusion must be erroneous."

"Erroneous?" Thalina echoed. He thought she was wrong?

"I can find no reference that there has been any Carrier of the Seed who was not mortal and humanoid in my records. They are unilaterally of biological origin and I am not."

She got to her feet then, knotting her belt and putting her hands on her hips as she came to stand before him. "Perhaps your records are incomplete."

"Perhaps so." He fixed her with a resolute look, one that made her want to claim him again. "I invite you to augment my records by providing the name of any Carrier of the Seed who was not mortal and humanoid."

"Troy is a MindBender."

"Also humanoid and mortal, independent of his skills."

"My father, King Ouros."

"Humanoid in one of his forms, and also mortal. That he is said to have a second form is not material."

Thalina frowned. "What do you mean he is *said* to have a second form? That sounds like you don't believe he can become a dragon."

"It is not a question of faith or religious conviction," Acion said. "I have never witnessed a creature shift shape before, king or not, and so I retain some skepticism that it can be done." He ran a hand over his head. "The biological complications inherent in a creature multiplying its size several times over as well as changing the shape and color of its body are daunting, to say the least. This can only cast doubt upon the assertion by dragon shifters that their kind is an ancient and primitive one."

"Haven't you ever seen any shifters?"

Acion shook his head. "This is why I would welcome the opportunity to observe one."

"But if you're the Carrier of the Seed, then I must be a dragon shifter princess." Thalina raised her hands, inviting him to look at her.

Acion shook his head again, and this time he frowned. "You have been constructed to resemble the princess Thalina, to be sure. I would have to be able to compare the strength of the resemblance in the presence of the princess herself, a situation which I find distinctly improbable given that I have been found to be an intruder in the palace..."

Thalina's temper flared. *Constructed to resemble the princess Thalina?* "Who do you think I am?" she demanded.

A man wise in the ways of dragons would have taken a warning from her precise speech and low tone, but Acion only spared her the barest glance and took her question at face value. "It is evident that you are an android created by a talented maker. That is the only reasonable conclusion given the available data. The quality of your simulated skin and sexual organs *is* remarkable in both detail and functionality. In fact, I doubt that either your skin or genitalia could be distinguished from the biological equivalent, and would welcome the opportunity to take a small sample back to the Hive for research purposes...

He wanted a piece of her for the Hive?

Thalina growled. "You're calling me a liar?"

"A liar?" Acion considered this, his eyes flicking. "I thought of your choice as adept management of information. When dealing with intruders, some deception is permissible, according to my programming and undoubtedly, yours." He halted and studied her, seeming to finally notice her reaction to his words. "You are vexed. This is irrational on your part," he scolded gently. "You should modify your understanding of my words in their context. I mean to flatter your maker, and truly, you shouldn't take offense easily, especially given your intended application."

"What intended application?" Thalina asked in that same quiet tone. A puff of smoke rose from her nostril and she knew her eyes were glittering coldly. She could feel the shimmer of the shift already vibrating in her belly and knew a pale blue light would soon emanate from her skin.

Acion was going to get his wish soon.

He blinked as if her question was unexpected. "It is highly probable that an android possessing such capability to mimic arousal and sexual satisfaction is intended for deployment amongst the sirens in the markets of Incendium. Perhaps they are to be replaced. The care taken in the manufacture of your sexual organs reveals the plan of your maker clearly. Surely you must be aware of that intent, or have deduced it for yourself. You do not seem to be lacking in computational powers." He shook a finger at her and smiled slightly. "In fact, to test your prowess against that of a male android is a most clever means of rating your performance..."

He had no chance to finish his sentence. The suggestion that Thalina was not just an android but one destined to provide sexual fulfillment to paying clients— and not a dragon shifter princess—only compounded his error of calling her a liar.

"I am the princess Thalina!" She roared as the heat of the change shot through her body, stretching her sinews and boiling her blood. "And I *am* a dragon shifter!" Acion fell silent and took a step back, his eyes moving faster than should have been possible. She knew he was gathering information.

Thalina would give him some data. She bellowed as wings grew from her back, as she grew a long tail, as her teeth became long and her talons longer. Scales sprouted from her skin and rattled as they covered her body. Her wings brushed the top of the chamber and her tail swept across the floor before she locked her gaze upon the offending android.

"As you see," she murmured, her deep voice making the floor vibrate. "The biological complications are easily overcome when you know how."

Acion stared at her. "But this is against all statistical probability and must be an illusion," he managed to say before Thalina breathed the torrent of flames in his direction that he so roundly deserved.

The first indication that Acion's conclusions were flawed was the way his companion began to glow, as if a blue light was emanating from her skin. She might have been lit from within, or radiant, in a way that he couldn't quite reconcile with his understanding of android abilities.

Her eyes seemed to have a fire burning in their pupils, too. Acion quickly searched his databanks for the possible reason for that glow. He considered that this might have been an augmentation from her maker, one he'd never witnessed before, and launched a search of sexual preferences on Incendium.

He'd barely begun that search when she became much larger. In the same instant, so quickly that he couldn't quite see their development, she grew wings, a tail, and dark green scales. Talons grew from her hands and feet, gold rippled over her belly, and her shape changed in the blink of an eye to that of a large dark green dragon.

Acion adjusted his reasoning to allow a total correlation between that blue glow and the individual emitting it being a dragon shifter.

On the cusp of change.

He sprinted for the door, but his reaction was too late and too slow, despite both being highly improbable individually and infinitely less so in combination.

The second indication that he had made a mistake was the lick of flames on his back. His shirt caught fire, his chausses dried instantly, and orange fire surrounded him completely. He tried to outrun the flames without success. He reached the wall all too soon and ran his hands over it, seeking a seam he could cut open. He heard the dragon roar. He was surrounded by the fire of her fury and knew the damage to his exterior membrane was extensive. He could smell it.

A reaction considerably more powerful than any fight-or-flight response he'd ever experienced shot through Acion's body, making him want to battle for his very survival. He couldn't find a seam in the wall. The saw in his index finger only created more sparks against the metal wall and didn't even scratch the surface. He couldn't run. He clawed at the edge of the sealed door, but the fire only got hotter. He couldn't see anything but flames, and he saw that the burn was spreading. He could smell the metal of his shell beginning to heat.

Acion calculated an escalating probability that each breath would be his last.

But the flames stopped.

The smoke cleared.

Acion opened his eyes. He looked back at the dragon, who was watching him as avidly as might be anticipated from a predator. Smoke still rose from her nostrils and her eyes glittered coldly. The floor was singed to black between them, but he was still intact.

He recognized that this was because she had chosen to let him be so.

Should he thank her?

The dragon took a step closer and Acion watched her warily, desperately searching his databanks for information about dragons. He had one, almost encyclopedic, reference, and scanned it rapidly. *The species Draconis is a large and varied group said to be one of the few creatures surviving from ancient times. Each subdivision has their own characteristics, from those associated with the elements—Firedrakes, Waterdrakes, Airdrakes, Earthdrakes—to those whose forms echo their favored environment—Frostdrakes, Mistdrakes, Emberdrakes etc. One folk tale declares that the fire breathed by all dragons was lit in the first of their kind by the light commanded to illuminate the dark chaos of the forming universe. Dragons are inclined to live a very long time and to breed very seldom—as a result, they tend to be comparatively rare amongst the life forms of the universe, and also broadly scattered. It is not unusual for a group of dragons to populate a specific area of the universe, assuming it as their territory, and over the eons to forget that others of their kind exist. They do have long memories but are inclined to discard details believed to be irrelevant to their survival in a process called "sifting and sorting." There has been speculation amongst biologists that sifting and sorting is an information management technique refined by dragons as even their capacity for memories is limited. A long-lived dragon may sift and sort more than once, or even do so routinely.*

The dragons of Incendium are a particular sub-species of Draconis called Mutatus, i.e. dragon shape shifters. The Draconis Mutatus has the ability to change from a dragon form to a humanoid form and back again. In rare cases, a specific dragon shifter may have the ability to assume additional forms. The abilities of one form do not necessarily transmit from one form to the

other—in human form, the dragon shifter can seldom breathe fire,
for example—but physical traits and injuries do carry between
forms. Generally, the dragon shifter has more abilities and more
powerful abilities in his or her dragon form, but this is not
necessarily the case.

The shape shifter dragons of Incendium usually mate with a
human of the opposite gender. The offspring of such mixed unions
are always dragon shifters. Rarely—as in the example of Queen
Ignita and King Ouros—a pair of shape shifting dragons are both
attracted to each other, destined mates, and able to conceive
offspring. This situation is always considered to be one of very good
fortune and the astrologers of Incendium spend considerable time
computing possibilities from this rare union. On other planets (like
Excandesco), it is believed that the mate of a dragon shifter should
always be a human who can't shift, in order to control the dragon in
the resulting child or children. The marriage of Ignita and Ouros is
an abomination to her sister Pennata, both because Ouros survived
his seduction and because their twelve daughters are dragon shifters
on both sides. Dragon shifters are not mature adults until they are
eighty-one years of age, and this is considered to be a lucky number
both among their kind and (usually) among those who live in their
company.

At the same time, Acion also gathered information.
This dragon's scales were deep green, but it was a
complex color, shading from emerald to obsidian on each
individual scale. The light played with the surface of the
scales, making them look iridescent. They gleamed. Her
belly, in contrast, looked as if it was made of pure gold, as
did her talons. Both shone. There were feathers adorning
her back and her tail, each of the same iridescent green as
her scales and they fluttered as she moved, catching the
light. Her eyes were golden brown, the same hue as that
of the woman he had believed to be an android, and it
was in her eyes that he found the glimmer of intelligence
that showed the commonality between the two forms.

No animal had ever looked at him with such

comprehension and awareness.

She was the princess Thalina.

Against every expectation.

She was a royal dragon shifter princess of Incendium. Acion sought new conclusions from this revelation, in the hope that one would provide some guidance. What had that reference to Excandesco meant? Acion searched again.

Excandesco is the planet where Queen Ignita was raised and where her blood relatives continue to reign. On Excandesco, the dragon shifters tend not to make enduring relationships. It is in fact customary amongst the female cousins of Queen Ignita to consume the Carrier of the Seed once fertilization of the egg has taken place. Her male cousins prefer to roast their destined mates once the egg has been delivered and secured. Ignita's sister, Pennata, is currently reigning monarch and holds the throne alone. Although the family of the sacrificed mate is showered with gifts and privilege, there is a tendency to hide if one is realized to be the Carrier of the Seed. Queen Pennata is reputed to be ruthless in uncovering the truth and is suitably feared by the occupants of her kingdom. Needless to say, the Excandescans don't believe in true love or HeartKeepers—a notable exception is Ignita and she frequently argues with her sister over this. In moments of marital strife, Ignita has been known to remind Ouros that he survives on her sufferance. In reality, she couldn't live without him and they both know it.

Acion straightened as his concern faded. He was confident in his ability to reason with any thinking creature. It was brute instinct that he found unpredictable. His information about dragon shifters, while limited, indicated that they were a logical species, if a passionate one, and he chose to discount the proclivity of the relations on Excandesco to devour their human mates. He wasn't human or mortal, so clearly was already an exception.

She *had* stopped the flames.

He stood and bowed, recalling that dragons expected

a measure of deference.

And rightly so.

"I apologize, Princess Thalina," he said. "My conclusion was deeply flawed, although it was a reasonable one, given the data available to me. It appears that I have been provided with incomplete information."

"I think you owe me a boon," Thalina said, and he found a correlation between her voice and that of the woman he'd pleasured. It was deeper and louder while she was in dragon form, but the inflections were the same.

"I would suggest that you might owe me one for breathing fire at me," he dared to say.

Thalina laughed. "That was just a warning."

Acion might have argued about the stringency of her warning, but it seemed to be a poor choice diplomatically. He'd wait until she was no longer a dragon before tabulating and presenting a list of his injuries.

His rejuvenation bots were still doing an inventory, which indicated that the damage was extensive. That he needed them for a second time in rapid succession was less than ideal, as they hadn't multiplied to their former numbers just yet.

"A warning for what?" he asked instead of pursuing that line of reasoning. He might have to complete his mission at less than complete functionality. He tabulated the effect of that upon his success and found it to be— unsurprisingly—diminished by thirteen per cent.

Thalina's gaze brightened and she took a step closer. She leaned down and Acion found himself treacherously close to those teeth. His back was against the wall and there was no option of retreating. He resolved that it was better to look confident and hold his ground rather than turn and run.

It was also easier to see what she was doing.

And he had nowhere to run, much less to hide.

"For daring to suggest that my favors are for sale," Thalina said, her gaze running over him. She frowned and he braced himself for another assault of flames. "You're more badly hurt than I expected," she continued softly, to his surprise. "Why are you so flammable?"

A miscalculation? How intriguing. "It is not in my programming to question my maker's choices."

If a dragon could look contrite, this one did.

"I apologize," Acion said again, because it seemed wise. "I have never encountered a woman of such passion as you showed and the conclusion I made about your role was erroneous."

"Maybe you haven't met the right kind of women," she murmured, then smiled. That only displayed more teeth and was less reassuring than she might have intended. "I apologize, too. I meant only to frighten you."

Acion found the husky tone of her voice alluring. Suggestive even. It made him think of her issuing an invitation as a woman and his body responded with an enthusiasm he found irrational, given his situation. He felt that heat again, even though his circuits should have been repaired. Had something changed?

He felt conflicted, which was entirely new.

Still, the dragon was waiting for his reply.

"There is a high probability of that premise being true, given that I have mostly been dispatched to serve Warrior Maidens on Cumae," Acion acknowledged. "They tend to be practical women, who like their pleasure delivered promptly and efficiently."

Thalina laughed again, surrounding him with a cloud of hot dragon breath. He smelled fire on her breath and noticed that what remained of his shirt—mostly in the front—was sparking again. He patted out the flames with his right hand, noting that the circuits were visible on that hand. The membrane had been fried away.

"I like to linger," she confided. "I think pleasure should be savored."

"An entirely reasonable perspective, given how rare pleasure is in our times."

She tilted her head to study him and her gaze brightened. "Is it rare?"

"In my experience, yes. I have been assigned to serve sexual pleasure only seven times since the completion of my manufacture, approximately once every two Cumaen years."

"Poor Acion," Thalina said and he was puzzled.

"I am neither lacking in funds nor fortune," he said. "I exist to serve and the schedule is not mine to determine."

The dragon glowed blue then, and he recognized the hue immediately. He kept his eyes open wide, determined to witness her transformation completely, and still, he barely saw it. In a flash, Thalina stood before him once more, a woman.

An enticing woman.

Who wasn't a siren or an android.

Who smiled at him as the flames in her eyes faded and died.

Relief flooded through Acion and his estimation of more peril to his shell diminished considerably, at least for the short term. His ratio of relief was irrational, given that she could become a dragon again at any moment, so he analyzed it.

He was *glad* to see her in her human form again.

Acion couldn't consider that unexpected response, because something about the glint in Thalina's eyes fed his arousal.

Again.

He had no capacity to read thoughts, but he could only conclude from her expression that she wished to be intimate again.

And he was more than willing.

Thalina closed the distance between them and swept her hand over him in one smooth caress. He watched her graceful movement, wishing that he had sensory input on more than his hands and face. Thalina frowned as she turned him and considered his back. "You need some repair, and it's my fault. I am sorry. What can I do to make it right?"

"Nothing. My system carries nanobots that are already being dispatched to assess and repair all damage."

"You did that already, didn't you?"

"Yes." Acion was impressed that she'd realized what was happening. "It was required after our intimate relations, though I cannot reason as to why."

"I don't understand."

Acion weighed the merit of confiding in her, and couldn't see why he shouldn't. "I felt a surge of unprecedented heat during our union."

She smiled and the sight made his heart skip. "Me, too."

"And it seared some of my circuitry. Repairs were necessary."

"That never happened before?"

Acion shook his head.

Mischief lit Thalina's eyes. "Perhaps it's a hazard of exceeding a pleasure factor of ten."

"That seems most reasonable." Acion found himself smiling in return. Their gazes clung and he had the curious sense that time had stopped. He was less aware of his injuries and more intent upon observing every detail of the princess Thalina. Her lashes were long and dark, and her hair had a slight curl. Her lips were full and he knew they were soft.

Welcoming.

Thalina's gaze returned to his back and shoulder, and he watched her fingertip run over the length of the damage. "But this is much worse. Can the nanobots repair it?"

"They will restore functionality to the best of their powers. The rest will have to wait until I return to the Hive." Acion already knew that functionality in his fingertips was impaired, which meant that the vibrator favored by the princess was inoperable. He didn't have a full range of motion on his right arm, and its strength was compromised to forty per cent of his usual power.

He launched calculations on the probability of success in his mission, given these constraints.

Thalina was watching him. "I can help."

Acion was astonished both by her conviction and her offer. "That is improbable."

"No." Thalina's confidence was complete. "I've been working with a clockmaker and building automatons under his supervision."

"I saw the dragon and the tower."

She smiled. "Did you like it?"

"It was clever. The children were pleased with it."

Thalina wrinkled her nose. "I think it's primitive, but the clockmaker can't see really tiny gears. We're working on a much more intricate one as a gift for my father. My idea. I have to do a lot of it myself, but it's very satisfying."

"How is the creation of an automated dragon satisfying?"

"It's predictable. It's logical. It does what it's programmed to do. I like that."

Acion realized they had something in common. "But you can see the small workings?"

"Dragons have superior vision." She sighed and considered his damaged arm. "If only I had my tools, I'd get you repaired."

Acion calculated her desire to fix his workings to be extremely high. Even better, he trusted her, a most curious sensation and one he couldn't fully explain. He tapped the hidden panel on his right thigh, which opened to reveal a full tool kit.

Thalina's eyes lit with pleasure and Acion felt pleasure in her surprise. "You are prepared for everything!" she exclaimed, then bent to examine a small screwdriver. "There are even spare parts." She led him back to the couch and urged him to sit down, moving with purpose. She surveyed the damage on the back of his shoulder. "Don't go into rejuvenation mode just yet," she warned. "I might have questions."

That was so perfectly reasonable that Acion could only agree.

CHAPTER FOUR

The king was displeased.

Ector, Captain of the Guard, knew the signs well enough. The cheerful mood of their last encounter was banished and the king's eyes had a telltale glitter as he reviewed the security video. The king was still, so still he didn't seem to be breathing, but Ector felt the tension rise in the small room that was the Vault.

Salvon was clever enough to stand behind Ector and keep quiet, for once.

"The princess proposed a plan, you said," the king invited, turning his attention from the recording and fixing it upon Ector.

Ector bowed and stepped forward, fighting his sense of unease. His royal overlords weren't unfair or cruel, but they did sometimes lose control of their tempers. With a dragon king, such a slip could result in great damage, however unintended it might have been. Ector feared that the well-documented temper of King Ouros would be roused to fiery splendor by the revelation that any of his daughters were imperiled.

"She did, your majesty. The plan was for her to interrogate the intruder in that first chamber, without any record or witnesses."

"How curious," mused the king.

"She implied that torture might be required," Ector

added. "And that it would be wise to have no record."

The king arched a brow.

Ector stepped forward. "If I may be so bold as to show you, sir, the thief came first to the gates, insisting that he had a gift for you."

"And was turned aside for lack of credentials," King Ouros said. "Presumably he found another way in?"

Ector nodded. "The princess was watching the security information from some other cameras." The king had responded to the summons so quickly that the Captain of the Guard hadn't been able to review them first. He replayed the sequences she'd watched for the king, then froze the image of the intruder crossing the river.

The king leaned forward as the sequence played again, emitting a low growl when the thief cut open the grate. He tapped the controls, zoomed in on the thief's fingertips, and replayed the sequence one more time.

"An augmentation, sir?" suggested Salvon. "I hear they are easily bought on some planets."

King Ouros magnified the image more and more, leaning close to the screen to examine a detail that Ector couldn't discern. "Not exactly," he said, his tone thoughtful. "I believe this thief is an android. Look at his eyes."

"That would explain the princess's interest," Salvon said and Ector wished his subordinate would remain quiet.

King Ouros gave the junior sentry a look so cold that he flinched. "She is very interested in automatons, but this situation is perilous." His voice hardened. "Scintillon's Law cannot be defied, even by a member of the royal family who is curious."

"Of course not, your majesty." Ector glared at Salvon, who dropped his gaze.

The king replayed Thalina's capture of the intruder,

then spun in the chair, drumming his fingertips. Ector wasn't reassured by the faint glimmer of blue around his royal person. "She changed the plan," the king said, his words clipped.

"Yes, your majesty."

"Then she must have had a reason. Thalina is practical."

"Because he was an android?"

"She would need more of a reason than that. An android might be able to threaten her person. If Thalina took a risk, she calculated the odds of survival to be in her favor. Why?" The king rose with purpose, evidently not expecting an answer. "Scintillon's Law is absolute and she knows it. Why did she spare the android?"

"Perhaps she wished to investigate his abilities before his annihilation," Salvon suggested. "Professional curiosity."

Ector closed his eyes as the king's gaze locked on Salvon. He expected little good, but Ouros cleared his throat and stood.

"I will go down there," he said.

"But, sir! I can send a guard and spare your majesty the inconvenience..."

Ouros silenced Ector by dropping a hand to that man's shoulder. "Not one who will see and smell everything I will see and smell, Ector," he said and the Captain of the Guard had to admit that was true. The king squeezed his shoulder a little. "You will accompany me."

"Yes, sir."

Salvon's relief was palpable that he was to be left in the Vault. Ector gave him some instruction on monitoring the situation, then followed the king, who was already striding down the corridor to the lower levels at a brisk pace. He brought a lantern, although the king didn't appear to need it.

"Did you memorize her direction, sir? Because I can link to the main system..."

"I recognize Thalina's scent, Ector," Ouros said. "Just as I recognize the scent of every citizen in my kingdom." He spared the Captain of the Guard a glance. "I could find any one of my children in the darkest night and locate my wife in the deepest abyss."

"Of course, sir." Ector couldn't smell anything except damp stone. He called up the link on his personal screen anyway, curious to see whether the king could follow Thalina's path unerringly. In fact, Ouros followed it so closely that he might have stepped in Thalina's every footstep.

The king halted in the storeroom, examining the wet mark on the floor, inhaling deeply and scanning the space. Ector shone the light around the empty room, noting the extinguished candle. He smelled the snuffed wick and thought the candle looked as it had been ground underfoot.

The king turned to Ector with an unexpected smile. "The Seed," he whispered, his eyes shining. "I will be a grandfather again, Ector."

Ector's mouth opened in surprise. "But you suspected he was an android, sir. Is that possible?"

"It must be. The scent of the Seed does not lie." Ouros moved quickly then, heading toward the sealed treasury. He leaned his ear against the door and smiled, just a little, then placed the flat of his hand against the smooth metal.

Ector couldn't see or hear anything, but the king's smile broadened.

"I wonder if it will be a boy or a girl," he said with undeniable pride.

"Is she safe, sir?"

"I feel the heat of recent dragon fire, Ector, and the stone still carries the resonance of a roar of pleasure. I believe my daughter is well and even pleased. How long has she been secured in the treasury?"

"Roughly an hour, sir."

"And her original scheme was to interrogate him for a day and a night?"

"Yes, sir."

"I wonder if she could smell the Seed even at such a distance as the Vault," the king murmured, then sighed rapturously. "I remember how beguiling the scent of my partner in the wind was."

"If you will excuse me, sir, if the princess had known about the Seed from the outset, there would have been no reason for her to create and then discard her original plan."

"You're right, of course, Ector. Thalina may have had a sense that it was imperative to intercept him. She might even have believed she could further her own fascination, at least until she was closer to him and smelled the truth." Ouros nodded. "Then she did the only responsible thing under the circumstances."

Ector frowned. "To take him into the Hoard, sir?"

"To isolate and sequester him until she obtained the Seed. Scintillon's Law commands that all androids shall be destroyed on sight." Ouros scanned the door. "He cannot be her HeartKeeper. He must be simply a vehicle for the Seed. Perhaps he delivers it for the HeartKeeper."

"Yes, sir."

"He cannot harm any of us, and he cannot be harmed, so long as he is in the Hoard. He is at her mercy. I suspect this is her plan."

"Except by you, sir."

"Exactly." Ouros nodded with satisfaction and left the portal then, heading back to the palace with confidence as Ector hurried behind him. "We will leave Thalina in her love nest for the night, to ensure that the Seed is harvested, then we will intervene at first light."

"That is less than the day and night she commanded, your majesty."

"It is, but I believe it would be best to surprise Thalina. My daughters can be stubborn and I don't want any complications. Ensure that there are tranquilizers prepared, Ector. Thalina will be protective and may need to be subdued."

"Full doses, your majesty?"

"No, she mustn't be injured. Requisition one dose sufficient to put her to sleep and divide it between three launchers. Even if only one hits, she will be slowed down."

"Yes, your highness."

The king smiled. "Fortify yourself, Ector. Thalina will not take well to a challenge to the Carrier of the Seed, and I don't doubt that his own power is considerable."

Ector swallowed. "What exactly do you mean to do, sir?"

"Capture and interrogate the android, as she originally intended, in order to discover the reason for his presence in the palace. I will have the so-called gift he has brought me and all of the truth, or he will pay the price." Ouros lifted a brow. "Then—or sooner if he defies my will—he will be destroyed, as decreed by the law of my forebear."

Which was why, Ector knew, the Seed had to be harvested first.

Being able to examine Acion's workings was the best gift ever.

Thalina peered inside his shoulder, carefully studying the mechanism before she touched anything.

"It's so beautiful," she whispered, her gaze dancing over the replicated tendons and joints, the tiny transmitters that emulated the nervous system, the synthetic muscles. She gasped in wonder as she focused on the connections between the mechanical, the electronic and the biological. "So elegant," she mused, never having imagined anything so wonderful could be manufactured. The integrations showed a wonderful attention to detail.

"You've never seen the workings of an android before?"

"Not one like you." Thalina frowned. "Actually, not one in reality at all." She tapped up a reference volume on her computer screen and showed it to him. "Just in Furton and Sluenz." She returned to her study, marveling all the while.

"An outdated reference," Acion scoffed. "Compare their notations on sensory receptors and the ones you can see in my hand."

Thalina did as he suggested and was astonished by the greater level of complexity in his hand. "Your maker is really skilled."

"My maker is always improving his designs and increasing our capabilities. I was given an enhancement just before this mission."

"Did you ever know someone named Arista?" she asked without thinking.

Acion became very still. "Arista?" he echoed, but Thalina sensed the name wasn't unfamiliar to him.

"My sister's friend and Sword Sister. A Warrior Maiden of Cumae. You're from Cumae. You must know her—especially since she was an android, too."

Acion said nothing.

"You *did* know her!"

"I neither confirmed nor denied as much."

"But your silence tells me everything. You would have either said that you didn't know her, or that the information wasn't available to me at this time." Thalina shook her head. "It doesn't matter. I can see why Gemma never guessed Arista's true nature. Any chance of meeting your maker?"

"The probability is very low. The Hive does not leave Cumae."

"I'd make a pilgrimage there to learn more."

"The Hive does not admit voyeurs."

Thalina laughed. "Is that what I am? I thought I was a fellow enthusiast."

Acion again said nothing. Thalina hoped he was considering how it might be arranged. She'd leave Incendium and even endure a jump to learn more about this technology.

"Wow," she whispered, peering even closer. Her view was magnified in steady increments, an ability that she used habitually but one that always astonished the clockmaker. "The replicated axons are almost indistinguishable from their biological counterparts!"

Acion stiffened a little. "I do not believe that is so."

"Well, you probably haven't looked inside your own shoulder recently," she teased, knowing better than to expect him to laugh.

He lifted his left hand so that the screen embedded in the palm was positioned over the back of his shoulder, and Thalina heard a click. The image was probably delivered to his brain because he didn't look at his palm before adjusting the position and capturing several more images.

"See?" she said, and he made only a low hum of acknowledgment. She leaned over him, indicating the image on his palm. "Am I right that this part of the joint needs to be replaced, and this simulated muscle tissue should be reconnected here?"

"Yes, but you should start with the connection, because the nanobots will complete the muscle repair once it's in place again." He paused for a moment, flicking a glance at her. "Are you certain you have the skill for this?"

"I am," Thalina said with a smile. "But you can watch

to be sure." She lifted his hand so that he'd have a good view. She smiled when the shoulder was illuminated and realized he had a light in the screen in his palm. "I need the Fraxon B hook," she said, and Acion reached into the toolkit in his thigh.

Thalina was more skilled than Acion could have expected from any biological organism. He added her attention to detail and precision to his growing list of attributes of dragons shifters, after passion, logic, compassion. This one, also, was honorable.

She was patient, too. She took her time with his repair, ensuring that each part was done perfectly before she continued. Perhaps this was the gift of her longevity. Her accuracy was impressive, and her determination to fix her own mistake was admirable.

Acion provided her with suggestions and information, releasing the nanobots in waves as she completed the larger repairs for him. All the while, he wondered.

What had happened to his neurons?

He knew with complete accuracy that they had no biological components. They linked to the biologically derived sensors in his face and hands, and moored the biological membrane that sheathed his body. They themselves were replicas. *Manufactured* replicas.

But the neurons in the image he'd taken of his shoulder looked different. How could that be? They pulsed in a different way, a less mechanical way. They moved with a fluidity that their mechanical counterparts couldn't echo. Was this part of his last enhancement?

They looked organic.

Thalina was right that they were almost indistinguishable from their biological counterparts. Acion had a strange sense that they might *be* biological.

But how?

Where had they originated?

Was this one of his improvements?

He couldn't help thinking of the heat that had raced through his body upon his sexual release, and the sense of being fried from within. Had that been a casualty of excessive sexual pleasure? But why would the nanobots have restored his neurons using a different design?

Acion would have liked to have discarded the observation, or discounted it, but the image of his own shoulder was vivid in his thoughts. He magnified it repeatedly, and found only confirmation of Thalina's observation.

What did it mean?

Did it have anything to do with these feelings he was experiencing?

More importantly, was he succeeding at the Hive's test of his new functionality, or failing? Acion felt uncertain about the result of reporting to the Hive, as he never had before. Thalina's so-called warning had given him a taste of his own end that was more concerning than any close call he'd had before. Was that part of his improvement?

His reasoning came to an abrupt halt when Thalina exhaled with satisfaction. "Done!" she said. "Or at least as done as I can be. Let me watch the nanobots."

Acion released them, then his eyes opened wide.

Not because Thalina dropped her hand to the back of his waist and leaned over him.

But because he could *feel* the weight of her hand, where he knew he should have no sensory receptors.

He felt the silk of her hair brush his back, too, and the light waft of her breath against his rapidly repairing skin.

"You are amazing," she whispered and he felt his heartbeat quicken.

What was she doing to him?

And why did it feel so very good?

This change was a matter to investigate!

Acion rolled over and sat up, raising one hand to cup her chin. He noticed the way she caught her breath, the quick dilation of her pupils, the flush that rose on her cheeks. Her eyes began to sparkle and her lips parted, as if she could read his inclination in his eyes.

Or maybe she read it in his reactions. Acion noted that his own respiratory rate had increased along with his pulse. He was filled with that new heat, and a buoyant sense of anticipation.

Yearning. Yes, it was yearning.

For the first time, he understood the compulsion biological organisms felt with regard to mating. Frequently. Repeatedly. He smiled and touched his lips to Thalina's, echoing the way she'd brushed hers across his own earlier.

The sensation was sublime. Evidently, the abilities of his receptors had been enhanced during the repairs. He initiated a check of his systems, learned that the repair of his exterior membrane was eighty-seven per cent complete and that strength in his right arm had been diminished by fifty-two per cent. Thalina had tried, but she evidently didn't know enough about his design to repair him completely. He couldn't blame her for that, but would have to accommodate that diminished ability in his reactions, at least until he returned to the Hive for further repair.

For the moment, there was this new sensitivity to explore. He kissed her again, lingering over the contact, tasting her quick exhalation.

The fleeting touch wasn't nearly enough.

Her gaze searched his, as if she sought to read his programming. "Will you pleasure me, twice in one Incendium day?" she asked, her voice husky.

"It is already negotiated," he said, hearing that his

own words were strained. "We made an agreement and I have seen a dragon now. You must have the second delivery of the Seed."

She laughed, which made her eyes sparkle. He felt anticipation of their union, one that could be measured in his body's reactions. He felt arousal as he had before, and knew that his biometrics were responding to the stimulus of experience with this woman.

It must be the promise of gathering more data about her and thus about dragon shifters that excited him.

Anything else would have been illogical.

He stood up and cupped her face in his hands, bending to capture her lips beneath his own. She rose against him, and he realized she was standing on her toes. He eased his fingers into her hair and deepened his kiss, appreciating how she returned his embrace, liking how she wound her arms around his neck and surrendered to him.

His yearning increased exponentially as their kiss became more passionate. She opened her mouth to him and he caught her close, lifting her against his chest and slanting his mouth over hers. She sighed, a wondrous sound, and murmured his name. One of her legs wound around his and she gripped the back of his head, demanding more, demanding all that he was willing to give. Acion closed his eyes, almost overwhelmed by sensation and wanting even more.

He spun and lifted her to the couch, following her down to its softness, their kiss uninterrupted. He lowered himself over her, trapping her beneath him, and she made a growl of satisfaction. Then her kiss became more demanding, her legs wrapping around him as she feasted on his mouth. Acion was enthralled. When they parted, her eyes were sparkling and her lips were redder.

"I thought you had to rejuvenate," Thalina said, her words husky.

"Touch me," he said by way of reply.

Her gaze dropped to his erection and she smiled. "I thought five was a resting state."

"The resting state is considerably surpassed. Touch me."

Thalina smiled, looking impish and unpredictable in a way Acion found remarkably alluring. "Let's start with that finger," she said, lifting his hand within hers.

"It was inoperable after the incident."

"Then, we'd better check the repair."

Acion slid back the protective cover on the finger tip, revealing the vibrator, and Thalina's smile broadened. She lifted it to her lips and he activated it, watching the way her eyes closed with rapture and her lips parted. She leaned her head back, eyes closed, as he slid his hand down the length of her throat. He let the vibrator touch her earlobe, the underside of her chin, the hollow of her throat. He traced a path along her collarbone to her shoulder, noting where she reacted most strongly, then cupped her breast in his hand. She still wore her clothing, but he touched her through the cloth.

Thalina gasped when the vibrator touched her nipple and he teased it, then pulled away her chemise to put the vibrator directly on her skin. He watched the nipple harden to a point, feeling a curious satisfaction when her body responded according to his plan. He did the same to the other, then Thalina pulled his head down for a kiss.

He determined that he was able to multi-task, even when her hands swept over his back, launching a fire through him. She twisted and giggled when the vibrator ran over her ribs, proving that she was ticklish, then caught her breath and parted her thighs. Her expectation was so obvious that Acion wanted to surprise her.

He followed the path of his finger with his lips, creating a trail of kisses. He captured one nipple in his mouth, and when he'd coaxed it to a perfect taut peak, he gave the same attention to the other. He could smell Thalina's arousal, and his own was beginning to demand satisfaction. He eased down the length of her, then settled between her thighs. He feasted upon her there, using his tongue instead of his finger to give her pleasure.

Thalina's gasp of delight, and the increase in her heart rate, proved that his technique was satisfactory. The way her hands moved over his shoulders kept him burning with that newfound desire, as well as determined to please.

She would remember the second delivery of the Seed. Acion would make sure of it.

Thalina liked how intent Acion was upon ensuring her pleasure. He could have been her personal android, perfecting his approach to ensure her complete satisfaction.

Not that it needed much improvement.

His technique was wonderful. He seemed to know exactly how to drive her wild and to be determined to do it as quickly as possible. There was something thrilling about his intensity and Thalina found her arousal increasing so quickly that she thought she might spontaneously combust. Her heart was racing. Her skin was on fire. She was wet and hot and ready for him, her blood boiling and her need beyond anything she'd experienced before. She found her fingers digging into his back and her legs wrapped around him, but Acion was relentless. He didn't push her over the edge but he didn't stop, either. She wasn't sure she could stand any more. She was writhing. She heard herself begging.

And then he used that finger.

As soon as the vibrating tip touched her clitoris, Thalina found her release. She shouted as the fire shot through her body and locked around Acion, holding him fast as she quivered and shook.

When she managed to open her eyes and catch her breath, he was watching her with such an expression of pride in his feat that she found it hard to believe he was an android.

"Were you satisfied?" he asked.

"Not quite," Thalina said. "I want more."

"You are voracious," he said softly.

"I'm a dragon princess," she replied, rising from the couch to shed her clothes. She liked how Acion studied each increment of skin as it was revealed. She liked that he looked at her as if she was a marvel to be investigated, as if he'd never seen her before, as if they hadn't pleasured each other so recently. It was exciting to have his attention so fixed upon her and she guessed that he was gathering information about dragon shifter princesses.

She was glad to be his object of study. His interest in her mirrored her interest in him and made her feel that they had much in common.

"I have a suggestion for you," she said and his gaze flicked to hers.

"Do you?"

"I think it's one that you're likely to accept."

He smiled, just a little, and her heart skipped. "How likely?"

"At least ninety per cent."

"And will that give you pleasure?"

"Yes."

"Then please tell me of it.

Thalina returned to him, sitting beside him and sweeping her hand over him as she had once before. This time, she heard him inhale sharply and knew that his arousal index was rising.

"I think you should investigate dragon shifters and document any discrepancies between dragon shifters in their human form and other humanoid women."

"An excellent suggestion," Acion said, reaching to cup one of her breasts in his hand. "You underestimated its appeal by at least eight per cent." His thumb slid over her breast and Thalina tipped her head back, feeling her nipple respond to his touch.

Then she remembered their conversation. "Well, there's another part of the suggestion, one you might find less attractive."

"So, the appeal of the entire proposition would be diminished once the less appealing part is factored into the end result. I understand." He bent and took her nipple in his mouth, tugging it to a taut peak and making Thalina shiver. He was so good at that. He flicked his tongue against the nipple, then looked up at her, eyes glinting. "Tell me the part you expect me to find less appealing," he whispered.

"I think the investigation should be reciprocal. You want to learn more about dragon shifters. I want to learn more about androids."

His gaze flicked and she knew he was calculating. "To what purpose?"

"I'm curious."

"The lore of biological organisms suggests that curiosity is a dangerous trait."

Thalina smiled. "That must be what I like about it."

He tilted his head, his thumb still moving back and forth across her nipple. "Why would you like a prospect of peril?"

"Because danger makes me feel alive."

Acion didn't respond for a moment. "Triggering the fight-or-flight response contributes to your awareness of your existence?" he asked, obviously uncertain of the merit of this conclusion.

"Experiencing sensation, taking risks, triumphing against the odds, feeling and enjoying and daring—these make me feel alive."

His hand dropped from her breast. "But that is irrational. How can risking your life unnecessarily make you feel alive?"

"It does, when I triumph."

"But what if you do not?"

"I'll have had one magnificent moment. That'll make taking the chance worth it."

"Even if it is your last moment?"

Thalina nodded. "Otherwise, I'd just be plodding through my life, safe and bored. I might as well be dead."

Acion stood up. He paced a few steps and she could almost hear his circuits humming, then returned to confront her. "I cannot accept this premise. You are not an irrational individual."

"Haven't you ever taken a risk?"

"All risks are calculated. Only those that are likely to have a favorable conclusion are undertaken."

"Ever wrong?"

He lifted a brow and she laughed.

"Of course not. Silly question. So, you've never really taken a chance. You've never really risked your survival for anything."

"Of course not. I didn't know that anyone did." His eyes narrowed. "Is this behavior specific to dragon shifters?"

"No. I think everyone does it to some extent." Thalina watched him, fascinated by the challenge she had unwittingly given to his programming. She couldn't resist the temptation, so leaned close to whisper. "If you could try anything, without concern for the probabilities of success, what would it be?"

He didn't answer for a moment and she wondered if he would.

Then he frowned.

"I would fly," he admitted, his words halting as if the

confession surprised him as much as it did Thalina. "I would climb to the highest mountain I could find and leap from its highest point, then fly. I like how it feels in a Starpod to soar over the land, and I have always thought it would be ideal to do that without the burden of a vehicle."

"Why?"

To her surprise, he looked discomfited again. "To feel free." He hesitated, then swallowed and Thalina thought of his comment about uploading his observations to a central processor. Was that what he did with the Hive? Did he feel trapped by that?

"I like the wind on my face." His words lacked conviction, as if he sought to convince both of them. Their gazes met for a moment and Thalina saw consideration in his eyes.

"Only on your face?"

"I am equipped with sensory receptors only in certain areas of my body. My face. My hands." There was doubt in his voice, and Thalina thought she knew why.

"I hope somewhere else," she teased.

"My genitals," he confirmed.

"So, you wouldn't really feel the wind over all of your skin."

"But I would like to feel it where I could." Acion shook his head. "But taking such a risk would be an irrational choice. I don't possess the necessary augmentations or programming for flight."

"What about swimming?" Thalina asked. "Diving into the ocean is similar, I think, to flying."

His eyes brightened. "You know this because you have done both."

Thalina nodded. "The feel of the water rushing past is similar to the sensation of the wind. Couldn't you swim?"

Acion shook his head. "My seals are sufficiently watertight only for surviving precipitation and for cleansing. To be immersed in water for any period of time would be detrimental to my condition." He licked his lips. "I would rust." Then he arched a brow, as if inviting her to laugh.

Thalina did. She hadn't heard him make a joke before. "So, you wouldn't risk it."

"To do so would be in defiance of my mandate."

"You exist to serve," Thalina remembered.

"And only my maker can determine when that service will end."

"So, no risky choices."

"It would be irresponsible."

"It might be fun." Thalina grinned. "What if I took you flying? Your maker would never know."

Acion laughed for the first time in her presence. "My maker knows all!" he countered. "Every impression and bit of data is shared with the maker."

"Even now? Even here?" Thalina didn't like the sound of that. "Does your maker know what we did?"

"Not yet. But the Hive will know all when my report is delivered."

"When will that be?"

"That information is not available to you at this time."

Thalina wanted to strike him. In fact, she poked him hard in the chest, so hard that he took a step back. "You need to stop saying that to me."

"I must obey my mandate."

"Can you keep any data out of your report?"

"I do not understand."

Of course, he didn't know how to lie. "Is it possible to make your report but omit to share certain details?"

"Like?"

"Like your observation that my genitalia were exceptional copies of their biological counterparts."

Color rose on the back of Acion's neck. "I can

correct the conclusion, but I don't believe it possible to completely delete it from my databanks." He frowned. "It is possible that such a detail wouldn't be passed to the Hive via a remote connection but as soon as I return to Cumae, all of my data is shared with the Hive. It is protocol."

And programming. "So, you can't lie to the Hive?"

"Why would I want to?"

It was amazing to Thalina that androids were banned from Incendium when it appeared that they were most likely of all beings to obey dragon kings perfectly and without question, a situation her father often loudly wished was his own.

That thought led to an obvious question. "What if you did something the Hive wouldn't approve of? Wouldn't you want to hide that detail from the Hive?"

Acion shook his head. "But that is impossible. I can only do what the Hive has designed and programmed me to do."

Thalina, once again, found herself determined to challenge Acion's conviction.

"What's under your other fingers?"

He opened his mouth to make his standard protest but Thalina placed her fingertips over his mouth to silence him. He swallowed and his gaze brightened. "Show me," she commanded, then replaced her fingertips with her mouth.

One thing was for certain—Acion's programming included a remarkable capacity for kissing. Thalina backed him into the wall, caught his face in her hands, and demanded even more.

The princess Thalina was insatiable.

If she continued at this rate, initiating intimacy every sixty-two minutes, Acion's entire lifetime total of sexual experiences would be doubled within four-hundred and thirty-four Incendium minutes, or 7.23 hours local time.

But that calculation did not include the actual time required to complete such intimacy. The first time, it had taken twenty-two minutes, so six more such intervals would add one hundred and thirty-two more minutes to his calculation, resulting in a total time required to double his lifetime experience of sexual union to five hundred and sixty-six minutes, or 9.43 hours.

That was well within the window of her request that they be secluded for a day and a night.

Acion should factor in the time required for his repair in the aftermath of their union and the curious heat that surged through his workings.

Thalina pushed him to his back and closed her mouth over him, a sensation of warmth and softness that made Acion close his eyes. He recalled her suggestion that intimacy should be savored, so reasoned he should added an increase of ten per cent to each successive period of intimacy...

Her tongue flicked across him. Her hand closed gently around him and she caressed.

And Acion couldn't remember what he had been adding together.

Or why.

CHAPTER FIVE

While Acion rejuvenated after their explosive second encounter, Thalina speculated on events outside the Hoard.

She'd abandoned her own plan, which meant that Ector would have summoned her father. She didn't blame him for defying her order—when situations changed and the welfare of a member of the royal family might be at risk, the guards' duty was clear.

Her father would have reviewed all available security recordings. She wished she'd said something aloud or even under her breath about the Seed, but maybe he'd look closely enough to notice her physical reaction and investigate further.

In fact, he must have done that, because no one had charged the doors.

Her father must have come down to the corridor and smelled the Seed himself. The scent would have been less powerful for him, and a little bit harder to detect, but if he'd known what he was seeking, Ouros would have found it. He had keen dragon senses, after all. Maybe he had even suspected the reason for her choice before investigating.

The fact that the Hoard hadn't been opened yet meant that Ouros had decided to give Thalina some time to claim the Seed. She was glad that her father had some faith in her ability to defend herself, but wondered just how much time he would allow her.

Because no door in Incendium could be secured against the king.

Not even that of the Hoard.

Especially that of the Hoard.

"You are thinking," Acion said quietly from beside her.

Thalina turned to him with a smile. "I thought you were rejuvenating."

"I have the capability to multi-task." He turned his head, and his bright gaze locked with hers. "Your pulse skipped. What do you fear?"

"Just gathering information?"

His gaze flicked, as if she'd surprised him. "Not simply that. I feel concern for you and your happiness." He frowned and licked his lips, his eyes narrowing as he repeated the words. "I *feel* concern."

"Isn't that in your programming?"

"Not to my knowledge. My systems were enhanced for this mission, though, and the precise nature of the upgrade was not explained to me." He lifted a brow. "It must be so to allow for ideal conditions during an experiment and no infection of bias." He nodded slightly. "I *feel.*"

"Do you feel anything more than concern for me?"

"Isn't that enough?"

Thalina laughed but Acion didn't.

He frowned. "It is my understanding that females prefer to believe themselves and their welfare to be of import to their partners."

Thalina propped her chin on her hand to watch him. "Don't males?"

Acion's gaze flicked. "Perhaps so, but my experience of intimacy with males, of either android or biological origin, is small to the point of nonexistence. As a result, I would be speculating upon their desires and doing so without any basis of reference."

"And what's wrong with that?"

"It would be in violation of my mandate. I am programmed to reason, not to speculate—or worse, to guess." He seemed to shudder.

"But you've never before been programmed to feel."

Their gazes locked and some force sizzled between them.

"No," Acion admitted quietly.

"What's it like?" Thalina asked.

"It is strangely consuming," he acknowledged. "I am aware of you, as if you were a target to be tracked, yet my inclination is protective." His features lit. "As if you were a treasure to be defended." He frowned again. "And yet, I have a reluctance to interfere in your situation, if such interference would be undesirable to you." His gaze met hers again. "I wish to ensure that you have your desires fulfilled. This *feeling* complicates decision-making significantly."

"What if my desires are at the expense of your desires? Or your mandate?"

It was clear that this troubled Acion. His gaze flicked rapidly and Thalina knew he was seeking a reference in his databanks. The longer his search took, the more convinced she was that he wouldn't find one.

"I don't know," he finally admitted, looking as surprised by that as anything so far.

"This is why biological organisms speculate," Thalina said gently, inviting him to do so.

He considered her for a long moment, then rose to his feet. She watched him pace, and knew that he was sorting and re-sorting the information provided to him. It was so interesting to watch him learn. She wanted to teach him everything she knew and see how far his programming allowed him to emulate a biological organism.

Could she help him to become indistinguishable from a man?

Could she hide him in open sight? She wanted to keep him with her in Incendium. She wanted him with her when her conception was confirmed, and she wanted him beside her when their child was delivered. He was so reasonable and reliable. Thalina knew that Acion was already stealing her heart.

Could he become her HeartKeeper as well as the Carrier of the Seed?

Would there be time to find out?

Thalina thought about her father again and anxiety rippled through her. Acion's presence on Incendium was a violation of Scintillon's Law. He would be destroyed, with no opportunity for appeal. Could she plea on his behalf? Would she have the chance?

She had to find a way. Acion might be an android but he was far more than a machine. Scintillon had been dead for eons. His edict didn't reflect current technology and Thalina was determined to challenge it.

She hoped she could do so before her father eliminated Acion. How much time did she have? She doubted her father would allow her an entire day and night. He'd just give her enough time to claim the Seed.

Which she'd done twice.

She glanced at the door, wondering how soon Ouros would appear.

Then she realized something. At least some of Acion's neurons were biological. She'd seen as much herself. How much else of him was biological? The combination of his composition must be why he could be the Carrier of the Seed.

Was he a cyborg?

But then, why had he been surprised about his neurons?

Thalina sat up. Was Acion changing in her presence? Was his rejuvenation process replacing damaged parts with biological ones?

Was that even possible?

What had been the exact nature of the enhancement he'd undergone before coming to Incendium?

What if the nanobots he now carried were building a different kind of tissue to replace whatever was damaged?

"You have made a conclusion that surprised you," Acion said, and she realized he was watching her. "Will you tell me of it?"

With her father likely to open the door at any moment, Thalina saw no reason to hold back. "What are the probabilities that your enhanced programming is turning you into a biological organism?"

"Zero." Acion spread his hands. "I have too many mechanical parts. While my body is sheathed in a membrane of biological origin, the interior can't be changed, much less undergo metamorphosis."

"Are you sure?"

His eyes flicked as he ran his calculations again. "There is a one hundred per cent certainty of this."

Thalina leaned closer. "What about those neurons?"

Acion frowned and fell silent.

In fact, he turned his back on Thalina and paced, a sign to her thinking that she was on to something.

"How much of you is biological?" she demanded.

"Less than ten per cent, although a more significant percentage of my construction emulates materials of biological origin. I can eat, for example, but the processing of food in my system bears little resemblance to that in yours."

"Because the nutrients in food that my body needs are useless to yours."

"Yes. Your body creates electrical charges with saline solutions and imbalances in such solutions between cells, for example, while similar functions in my system are triggered by actual electrical charges."

"Then how do you rest and recharge? Don't you need an electrical source?"

"Once androids did have such requirements, but the Hive was driven to free us from such restraints. I have a variety of systems that harvest energy wherever it can be found." He ticked his fingers. "Sunlight is the most easily converted, although artificial light will also work. I have processors to convert wind into power as it moves across my skin, as well as the ancient mechanisms for simply appropriating electricity." He opened two fingertips on his left hand, revealing two of the universal connections for electrical systems there. He tilted his head to regard her. "Why do you ask these questions?"

"What makes you think I have a reason?"

"My experience of you shows that you are rational and logical." His words pleased Thalina enormously. "I calculate a high probability that you are collecting data in order to test a theory."

"Or to solve a riddle," she said. "I'm trying to figure out how you could be the Carrier of the Seed."

Acion raised his brows. "I thought this was a deception on your part to seduce me and test your systems, but as my theory was incorrect, this conclusion must also be." His eyes flicked. "It is irrational. Are you certain of my role?"

"Yes."

He pursed his lips. "Could I have been designated as a receptacle and delivery mechanism of the Seed by the true Carrier?"

"Maybe." Thalina thought about this. "But when you rejuvenated, didn't you make more?"

"I made more, as you say, but am not certain it contained the Seed you seek."

"I am." Thalina folded her arms across her chest. "I

can smell it."

Acion nodded and paced again, and she liked that he trusted her conclusion even though he couldn't verify it himself. "Have there ever been other Carriers who were not biological?"

"No."

"You speak with great certitude, yet the population percentage of dragon shifters on Incendium indicate that there are not only a significant number of your kind currently living here, but that there have been far more in the past. How can you truly be certain of the nature of the partner of each and every one?" He closed his eyes, then opened them again. "I would estimate the number of dragon shifters who have lived on Incendium to be in excess of three hundred individuals, and there are dragon shifters elsewhere in the galaxy as well."

"But on Incendium, they can't have mated with androids because of Scintillon's Law."

He was silent for a moment, searching. "I have no reference for this legal statute."

"What?" Thalina was on her feet, furious on his behalf. "The Hive sent you to Incendium without telling you that androids are banned here?"

"Banned?" Acion's eyes narrowed.

"And if found, terminated, neutralized, or destroyed immediately, with no appeal. That's Scintillon's Law."

Acion ran a hand over his head, a sign of concern that Thalina had noticed earlier. "Excandesco," he said quietly, his gaze locking upon her.

Thalina didn't immediately understand. "My cousins rule there. Why?"

He lifted a finger. "You decreed one day and one night of seclusion for us, in order to claim the Seed. What will you do to me now that you possess it?"

"I'd like to stay with you." She took a step closer to him. "I'd like you to stay with me."

"That is not my mission."

"Well, maybe your mission should change. Maybe you should *choose* to stay."

"That would be a violation of my programming and my mandate. I am to complete my mission and return to Cumae immediately. I have rented a Starpod to ensure my swift return to the starport where I will find passage to Cumae." Acion considered the door. "But the probability of my success is vastly diminished, given this new information about Incendium's law." He fixed her with a look. "If androids are banned, then why aren't reference volumes about them also banned? You have several and are familiar with their contents."

Thalina blushed. "My sister, Anguissa, got them for me."

"How?"

Thalina sighed. "Well, she was always a good negotiator, so when she came of age, she joined a trading mission. I don't think she's been home for more than a few days in a row since."

"And how old is this sister?"

"Don't you know?"

He grimaced. "My brief is incomplete."

"Anguissa is younger than me but not by much. She's been roving the galaxy for over three hundred years. We tend to think she can find and acquire anything."

"A most useful individual to know." Acion seemed thoughtful, and Thalina was pretty sure she knew why.

"Do you think the Hive knew about Scintillon's Law?" she asked gently.

"The Hive knows all," Acion said without hesitation. "My fate is clear."

"I'm going to talk to my father..."

Acion shook his head. "Perhaps you will not be directly responsible for my demise. But when those doors open, I will be destroyed." His tone was flat but she felt a desolation in him.

"Not necessarily," she protested.

"Do not pursue irrational conclusions now. Your clear thinking is much of what I admire about you. Probabilities are very high that plans are being laid now." He cast a glance at her, a small smile curving his lips. "And yet, there is a benefit to be gained in this conclusion."

"How so?"

"I understand your impulse as I did not before. I am surprised to acknowledge that I would rather try to fly and fail, to have that experience of vitality, than to simply face my destruction." He licked his lips. "I would have liked to have known what it felt like to take a chance."

Thalina's heart clenched and she found it hard to take a breath.

He tilted his head to regard her again. "Are you certain about the Seed?" he asked quietly. When she nodded, he continued. "And that it will bear fruit?"

"That's the point of the Seed. That's why its scent calls to us."

"How curious it would be to father a child," Acion mused. "I should have liked to have had that experience, as well."

Somehow she had to wring a legacy from her time with Acion, a greater legacy even than having his child. The fact that Acion could feel and that he had concern for her desires mitigated her own fear that he would be obliged to report anything he learned to the Hive. He might not even have the opportunity to make that report.

It was highly improbable that there would be another android on Incendium anytime soon. Thalina had to take advantage of the opportunity, even though it wasn't perfect.

"Help me," she invited, wanting to take the desolation from his expression.

"Help you? In what way?"

"There's a riddle I can't solve. Maybe you can." She took a breath. "Maybe you can help me to understand something." She smiled. "I'd like to have a story about you to tell our child."

He blinked. "There it is again," he murmured, as if she wasn't supposed to hear.

Thalina did though. "What?"

Acion raised a hand to his chest. "A new experience I have found in your presence. I *yearn*, even though I know my desire will never be."

Oh! His words and his acceptance of this brought tears to Thalina's eyes and fed her resolve to somehow change her father's mind. She got up with purpose, dressed and went to the vast wall of storage cabinets. She felt Acion watching her but he couldn't memorize this code.

The lock was keyed to her DNA and her voice, and so finely tuned that it could detect any stress beneath an involuntary utterance.

She placed her hand on the panel and felt the prick on her palm.

"Scintillon," she murmured, her voice low and soft.

There was a delay, a moment long enough for Thalina to doubt the result, a pause long enough for Acion to come to stand behind her. She noticed that he had his hand on his belt and she was aware the quickening of his defenses.

Then the panel slid open and she smiled at his gasp of surprise.

There was something very satisfying about challenging Acion's conclusions and projections, as carefully tabulated as they were.

Who or what was Scintillon? Acion had no reference for that word, which only increased his irritation with the inadequacy of his brief. How could the Hive have omitted to inform him of the risk to his own survival on Incendium?

How could the Hive have been so irresponsible?

The Hive was not irresponsible and Acion knew it. This law must be part of a greater plan. Was it the Hive's intent to test these enhancements then eliminate the android in question? Would Acion's success in adapting to whatever changes were made in his system determine the chance of his survival? Acion found it inconvenient that his strength was diminished and he feared that these newfound feelings would undermine his decision-making processes. He thought of Arista's murder and how he had doubted when he heard of it that she could be so surprised by an attacker.

Had the Hive planned her demise? Or allowed it? Had Arista been instructed to allow it? Acion remembered passing her that last time he had entered the Hive. He had been allowed to see her there because the Hive had wanted him to know that she was an android, too. It was also probable that there was a connection between her report and his assignment. Perhaps she had tested the enhancements first.

And when he'd been released from the process of gaining his enhancements, Arista had been known to be dead.

Or eliminated.

Acion calculated the probability of his own future following a similar path to be in excess of eighty-six per cent, given the new data offered by Thalina. Once he would have repeated that he existed to serve, but on this day, he felt a dull glow of rage. He had been used and even though that was his purpose, he resented it.

He wanted to rebel against the scheme of the Hive, which was so treasonous and unexpected that he refused to consider it. On one hand, he had to admit that these feelings compromised the fulfillment of his assignment. On the other, he already couldn't conceive of being without them—or sacrificing them.

Oh, he yearned for far more than was his due.

He wanted a future.

With Thalina.

Acion forced himself to dismiss these impulses. Instead he watched Thalina, intrigued by what else she might show or tell him. He wanted to savor every second in her presence.

He saw the drop of her blood on the panel when she lifted her hand away and watched the panel absorb it, as if it were made of some substance other than the metal it appeared to be.

The notion was fleeting, because the panel folded back. It kept folding, rolling away behind itself until an entire chamber was revealed. Thalina stepped into it with a confidence Acion did not share. It could be a trap. Well aware that his moments were limited, he was determined to defend every last one of them for as long as possible.

He followed her warily, surveying the numbered panels which were clearly doors to repositories. His survey revealed that there were eighty-one of them, ranging in size from that of the dice for gambling on Xanto to several large enough to contain men taller than himself. Acion felt the skin tingle on the back of his neck and turned in place to gather more detail.

It was clear that Thalina was familiar with this place. She counted the row of the smallest panels, then tapped the seventh one. It opened to reveal a small silver ball, about the size of his thumbnail.

Acion stared. The probabilities were extremely high—in excess of ninety-nine per cent—that it was a Cumaen *memoria*.

But what was it doing here?

"You know what it is," Thalina said without surprise.

Clearly, she'd learned to read his expressions. "I thought you might."

"It is a *memoria*, a recording device made on Cumae, or at least, it very strongly resembles one."

"I knew it!" Thalina said with satisfaction. She waved it at him. "This holds the key to everything. It has to."

"But how could you formulate such a conclusion?"

She smiled, that confident smile making his chest tighten in a new and not entirely unpleasant way. There was much to admire about this dragon princess. "What do you think the Hoard is?"

"A safe room. A place of refuge and final defense. A treasury."

Her eyes sparkled. "But what is the treasure?"

Acion surveyed the numerous panels. "Gems? Precious metals? Rare materials?"

Thalina laughed. "Yes, but that's not the heart of the Hoard." She watched him, eyes sparkling in a way that distracted him from their conversation, then leaned closer. "Knowledge is the real prize," she whispered. "The greatest valuable in the universe."

She left the chamber then, and Acion followed her. "It is not typical of biological organisms to value knowledge above all else," he was compelled to note. "And dragons are said to be particularly fond of physical wealth."

"Which just proves that you can't believe everything you hear." She cast a teasing glance his way. "Or give credit to rumor in your calculations." Before he could agree, she held out her hand, the *memoria* on her palm. "Do you know how to make it work?"

Acion saw no reason to disguise the truth. "*Memoria* are typically used by the Warrior Maidens of Cumae, to leave information for those who follow, in case their mission fails and must be completed by another."

"They don't just report to the Hive?"

"The vast majority of Warrior Maidens are not androids."

"But some are. Interesting." He was startled that she made the inference so quickly and realized he shouldn't have revealed as much information. She brandished the *memoria*. "How is it activated?"

"Warrior Maidens train together and choose a companion from the ranks of their fellows called a Sword Sister. A Sword Sister is obliged to finish any incomplete missions of her partner, and so in the vast majority of cases, the *memoria*'s action is triggered by the voice of the Sword Sister uttering a word known as the code by only those two persons."

Thalina considered the small silver ball. "I think this belonged to my forebear, the dragon shifter who founded the line of kings of Incendium."

"Scintillon," Acion guessed.

Thalina nodded. "My father is the seventh son to reign as king, a direct lineage from Scintillon. Father to son to son, etc."

"Which would make Scintillon your great-great-great-great-great grandfather."

She smiled. "Exactly." She took the *memoria* between finger and thumb. "He was reputed to be brilliant and mechanically inclined. He built clocks and automatons. I could like him, but he was the one who made androids illegal on Incendium."

"Scintillon's Law," he guessed and she nodded. Acion was puzzled. "But why? Such a man would be most likely to discern our usefulness."

"Exactly," Thalina said, waving the memoria at him. "I could never solve that riddle. What if the answer is in here?"

"It is possible, maybe even probable, but as a king, he would have no Sword Sister."

"Maybe not technically. You say a Sword Sister

finishes what her partner can't. What else does she do?"

"Sword Sisters defend each others' blind spots. Indeed, they often fight back-to-back."

"Fructa," Thalina said and strode to another panel in the wall of the chamber. Again, she laid her hand upon it, but this time, the panel opened to reveal a single smaller repository. A small chip reposed within that space.

"Fructa?" Acion asked. He must complain to the Hive that his brief was sorely deficient for this mission. Even if that had been intended to be part of his test, he believed that he was compelled to respond at a much lower performance level than gave him pride.

"His wife. Mother of his sons."

"She defended his back?"

"Time and again. Incendium was often attacked in its early days as a kingdom. The forebears of the Regalians battled my forebears for control of the planet and, thanks to their deceptive and violent inclinations, were ultimately exiled to a planet of their own."

"But still within your system."

"Where do you think the expression comes from to keep your friends close and your enemies closer? My ancestors wanted to keep an eye on the Regalians."

That was a logical choice, in Acion's view.

Thalina picked up the chip. "Scintillon died, after reigning for two hundred and six years. His third wife, who wasn't a dragon shifter but was his HeartKeeper, ruled after him for another five Incendium years, finishing what he'd started and acting as regent."

"I will speculate that their oldest son was not yet eighty-one Incendium years of age."

Thalina smiled. "Good guess. She ensured Rubeo claimed the throne and that his brothers supported him, and then she died."

"Because the task was completed." Acion nodded. "There are strong similarities between these events and the traditions of Sword Sisters."

"My thinking exactly. Let's listen to Fructa, and see if the *memoria* likes her voice."

Acion followed Thalina across the chamber to a portion of the wall that he had believed to be patterned. On closer inspection, the patterns revealed themselves to be portals and receptors. Thalina fitted the chip into the receptacle shaped to receive it and a woman's voice emanated from the walls. Though she spoke the common tongue, her accent was heavier than that of the current inhabitants of Incendium and Acion had to adjust his filters to ensure he didn't miss any detail.

"We are gathered for the saddest of occasions, to celebrate the life and mark the death of our exalted king and my beloved husband, Scintillon the Bold. There are many here today who will speak of his life and his accomplishments, his connections and influence both on Incendium and in the galaxy beyond. My story of Scintillon is rooted here, in Incendium's main city and, even closer, in my own heart. Most of you know the more public part of our story, how I came to this palace first when my father, a knight in the service of the king, brought me to the palace to see my swordsmanship improved. I was disguised as a young man. Most of you know that I drew the king's eye first in tournament, when I triumphed in battle and boldly declared the truth of my gender. Most of you know that these events immediately occurred before the last attack of the Regalians, which followed that tournament. I can't explain to you the shock of that moment, the sensation of celebration shattered by an unprovoked attack. We were besieged when it was least expected and sorely beset. My father was cut down in defense of the king. I saw him fall and knew he wouldn't move again. I was his only child, I held a blade, and so I stepped into the void to defend the king. *My* king. Scintillon and I fought back-to-back on that day, and the Regalians were narrowly defeated. That was the day they were exiled, catapulted to their own planet with no means of leaving it, close enough to watch yet sufficiently distant to pose no threat to Incendium. It was eighty-two years ago this year." There was a pause. "It was the day that King Scintillon doffed his gloves, took my hand in his and invited me to celebrate our victory by becoming his wife. I was astonished but not so foolish as to decline. I knew nothing about the Seed in those days. I knew nothing about HeartKeepers. I knew I loved the king because he was my king, because I had been taught to love the king, because this king was good and fair and honorable. I had no notion of the happiness that would be mine, because I had bound my life to that of my HeartKeeper. Scintillon, so much older and wiser than me, knew exactly what he was doing and precisely the path he placed us upon. I thanked him for that gift every day that we were together."

She cleared her throat, silencing the bit of applause. "But few of you know the challenges we faced privately, and I will tell you of one because it colors the future that we share together in the absence of Scintillon. I wish I had met Scintillon sooner. I wish he had died later. My desire is selfish because it makes me ache to be parted from him, his kindness, his passion, his absolute sense of justice, his ability to make me smile no matter the situation. But his passing has import for a matter of state as well. Our son and Scintillon's legal heir, Rubeo, is seventy-nine years of age. He has not yet come of age according to the counting of his kind, which was his father's kind, which means that I will act as regent for the next two years as he completes his preparation for his role as king and is readied for his coronation. I am proud of Rubeo and I know he will do his father's memory credit, but the death of the father makes me recall the death of our first son, Torris."

As she said the name of her lost son, the seam became more visible on the *memoria*. It didn't open, but Acion reasoned chances were very good that this was the word that would release its secrets. He was glad he was recording the audio.

Fructa continued. "Our first son would have been eighty-two if he had survived the hatching of his natal egg. Ever since the morning that I held my lost son in my arms and feared that the future had been lost, I counted that as the darkest day of my life. Ever since the night that they finally took him from me and I wept from the depths of my soul, believing I had betrayed my husband's hopes and my own, I have counted that as the darkest night of my life. But on that morning, I had Scintillon by my side, resolute and intent upon securing the future of Incendium. On that night, I had Scintillon holding me close, strong and determined to do all in his power to keep Incendium's future bright. I had a spark in the darkness, the light that was my husband and his faith in the future, his conviction that justice and honor could only prevail. And so it did, even though my faith faltered when the days passed with no new conception. And so it did, because Scintillon would not surrender when he knew the greater good could be served. And so it did, when Rubeo broke free of his natal egg and gave a roar that was said to have been heard all around the planet of Incendium. We had three more sons, each stronger than the last, and Scintillon's legacy was assured."

The crowd applauded a little in the background.

"Today, I stand before you on what should be the darkest day of my life, for there will be no spark to light this darkness for me. The spark of my husband's will still burns in my heart though. Its brightness will never fade, not so long as I draw breath, and this is his gift to me. He granted this gift of hope to me so that I could finish the work of ensuring his legacy. I will do whatever is necessary to see my son crowned King of Incendium in two years time. I will sacrifice whatever must be cast aside, be it a treaty or a truce, if Incendium is threatened in what might appear to others to be our moment of weakness. The fire of the first King of Incendium burns hot in my breast, and his love of justice will be defended as fiercely as if he stood beside me. Make no mistake, once again, Scintillon and I fight back-to-back to secure the future of Incendium."

There was a roar of approval on the recording, as an enormous number of people cheered and hooted, clapped and stamped their feet. Acion heard several shout "Praise to Queen Fructa!" then the call was taken up by the crowd.

Thalina touched a finger to the console and the cheering was silenced.

Acion stepped past her and played the recording made on his own palm, accelerating through the speech until Fructa reached her dead son's name. He amplified the output and placed his left hand over the *memoria* in Thalina's hand, so it was closer to the speaker.

As if Fructa whispered to it.

At the word "Torris," the device began to spin.

Thalina was shocked to see the small sphere spin of its own power, split in half and open. The beam of light emanating from its interior was also a surprise, but the quality of the hologram it projected was far better than she'd expected.

A king lounged on his throne before her, both existing only in the hologram. He had silver at his temples and in his beard, but still looked vital. She thought of warriors who aged but didn't stop fighting and would have guessed that he was still fierce in battle. There were scars on his hands and one on his cheek, but she recognized the dragon in his eyes. She supposed there was a faint resemblance between his features and that of her father.

"Your forebear," Acion said. "The bone structure of the face has correlations with yours." He calculated and she looked at him. "Stronger with your father, perhaps due to gender differences."

"Another king," the king in the hologram mused, his voice a deep rumble that hinted of banked fires and glowing coals. Acion and Thalina watched and listened. "That can be the only reason I've been set loose again." He smiled a little, as if amused by his own joke. "I hope there is another king, a long line of kings, an empire in Incendium, and a future filled with prosperity and good fortune." He inclined his head. "I wish all of this for you, King of Incendium in future, and wish also that you are the fruit of my Seed. I like continuity because I understand the power of stability."

He braced his elbow on the arm of his throne and propped his chin on his hand, surveying Thalina as if she truly did stand before him. She fought the urge to curtsey. Acion did bow. "And now, you, newly crowned king, are following the dictates laid before you, one of which is that you will watch me. That is a good sign for the future, in my view. I tend to prefer kings and emperors who follow the laws of their own domains. The edict that has led you to me is Scintillon's Law, of course, for it is the cornerstone of my legacy. I don't doubt that you would like to find a way to dismiss it or ignore it. Even in my time, androids have their appeal and I can only imagine that will increase. They can diminish labor. They can assume tasks that are risky for mortals. They can do our dirty work, and they can work longer and harder. They are economical beyond the initial cost of creation, often operate cheaply, and the cost of their construction can be mitigated with economies of scale." Thalina saw Acion nod agreement with all of these arguments. "And yet, *and yet*, I have outlawed them forever in the kingdom I founded. My law is the foundation of the government in Incendium and it decrees that no android shall be tolerated on the planet of Incendium or its governed territories. It states absolutely that every single android that ever sets foot on Incendium must be destroyed, without delay or appeal or exception."

Thalina saw Acion's eyes narrow.

"Didn't you know?" she whispered.

He shook his head. "Not until you told me."

"Didn't you have a brief?"

"This detail was not included. The brief noted that androids were uncommon on Incendium. There is no mention of Scintillon's Law."

"So, did the Hive not know, or did the Hive decide to put you at risk?" she dared to ask.

Acion frowned and gestured to the hologram. He folded his arms across his chest, and she would have bet that he was feeling something new and unwelcome.

"Why?" Scintillon asked. "Why would a king of supposedly clear vision lay down such an edict and structure the law of his kingdom in such a way that it could never be challenged? You might think I did it out of ignorance or superstitious fear." He laughed a little. "But that can only be because you don't know me." He confronted Thalina again and she straightened as if she was being interrogated. "I did it out of knowledge."

"Knowledge?" Acion echoed, skepticism in his tone.

Scintillon rose to his feet regally and gestured to the walls of the Hoard. "I have left a legacy of information, although there is no telling how it is stored by your time. It includes extensive documentation of our own robotics laboratories here on Incendium. Yes! We built androids. They were of the most highly developed of their kind, so we kept their development secret. We wanted to know how much progress we could make in simulating the thought processes of organic creatures. We wanted to know how perfect an android we could create."

Scintillon took a few steps, then turned back. "The answer is that we made an excellent one. We made the best androids ever known. They were so remarkable that even I—with my keen dragon senses—could not distinguish between a human warrior and an android one. The lead engineer himself could not distinguish the creatures of his manufacture and the naturally born warriors in our service. And this was all to be celebrated, until they began to think for themselves."

Acion was very still.

"They exceeded their programming and in so doing, became impossible to control."

Acion caught his breath. "Which undermined their usefulness," he murmured.

Scintillon nodded as if in agreement, although he had to be nodding in agreement with his own argument. "There came a point, just a few years ago, when the androids ignored their assigned mandate and made their own choices. While this was a triumph, it was also a problem, because we had discovered no means of creating the equivalent of a moral code in an android."

He held up three fingers, each adorned with a ring. "There were three incidents behind the development of this law." Scintillon waved his first finger. "One android stood guard during the interrogation of a Regalian rebel and became convinced of the merit of the rebel's cause. He slaughtered all of those in service to Incendium in that interrogation chamber, freed the rebel, helped him to escape, and joined the Regalian cause. They made great gains with his assistance, until he was incinerated by my two youngest sons."

Scintillon held up his second finger. "We were assured that the mutation had been contained and that the programming responsible for it was removed from all others. You can guess already that this was wrong. The second witnessed the destruction of the first android, resolved that my sons had acted unjustly and attempted to assassinate one of them during the night several weeks later—despite having been reprogrammed. The malfunction could not be recalled and the lack of a moral code meant that the android's vengeance could not be stopped. Again, the rogue android was incinerated and again, the engineering program came under scrutiny."

The king paced. "They said they had resolved it. They said we were safe. It seemed as if all had been resolved, for the androids were gathered and sequestered beneath the laboratories. They were completely reprogrammed and tested repeatedly. The edict was to ensure their absolute reliability before releasing them again. Instead, they revolted, outwitting their developers and attacking Incendium from within. We hunted them down and incinerated them, every last one, in a battle more bloody than those of our early days. My two younger sons, the ones who had felled the first rebel, were among those lost in the carnage. When it was done, and Incendium was a pale shadow of what it had been, I created my law and ensured it would hold for the duration of Incendium." He leaned closer, his eyes gleaming with intent. "There can be no negotiation. There can be no tolerance, because there can be no trust. Do not be so foolish as to try to undermine my law. It will cost you everything, far more than the crown, far more than the kingdom. My two sons are dead too soon, because I trusted where trust was not deserved." Scintillon fixed them both with a lethal glare, one that showed the dragon ascendant in his eyes, then disappeared abruptly.

Thalina didn't know what to say.

The *memoria* closed with a whirr and spun in her palm before stilling once again.

CHAPTER SIX

I don't think he's right," she said quietly.

Acion gave her a cold look. "We both know that doesn't matter. How much time is left until your deadline?"

Thalina checked the computer interface on her arm. "Nine hours."

"And what do you consider the probability of your father allowing you all of that time?"

Thalina wasn't startled that their reasoning followed the same path. "Almost nonexistent. He'll want surprise on his side. It's his favorite tactic." She frowned. "But he'll want to make sure I've claimed the Seed, so he won't interfere too soon."

Acion watched her, waiting.

"Aren't you going to calculate a probability?"

"Given the lack of information about the nature and habits of King Ouros in my brief, such a calculation would require so many assumptions as to be useless."

"You sound bitter."

"Chances are very good that I have been used for the benefit of others, with no consideration for my own survival. Although I exist to serve, I find the lack of disclosure in this case to be...irritating."

Thalina smiled. "Only irritating? I'd be a lot more than that if someone sent me to die without telling me."

Acion's eyes flashed and Thalina understood his reaction very well. "Angry, then," he said, his tone of voice so controlled that his claim was hard to believe.

"Angry? You *feel* angry?"

Acion nodded.

"Are you programmed for such emotional reactions?"

"I thought not. Perhaps this is the enhancement at work."

Acion nodded again. "Undoubtedly." He smiled, a little bit sadly. "And I can compute the reasoning behind the destruction of an android who has undergone these enhancements. It is logical, since the evolution of feelings in the system must necessarily compromise the android's ability to fulfill its assignment or mandate."

"How?"

"Already I consider the merit of surrendering the gift intended for King Ouros to you, even though my quest is to place it directly in his hand." His gaze met hers. "Because I trust you."

"Oh!" Thalina felt herself flush with pleasure. "How is that a bad thing?"

"I might be wrong in so doing. I might be persuaded to do so by your other charms."

"I have other charms?" she asked, wanting to hear him say it aloud.

"You have an abundance of them," Acion admitting, his eyes glowing as he surveyed her. "You are clever, logical, honorable, beautiful, passionate, surprising, strong, precise, and patient." He paused. "Though that is not necessarily the order of importance of those attributes."

Thalina stepped closer to him, placing her hand on his shoulder and caressing him. He closed his eyes and caught his breath. She felt his heartbeat increase and when his eyes opened, they glittered in a new way. "And I find you clever, logical, honorable, handsome, passionate, surprising, strong, precise, and patient," she repeated. "You're stealing my heart, Acion," she whispered. "I've never met a man so perfect."

He shook his head, apparently at a loss for words. "I'm not a man, Thalina," he reminded her.

"You are to me," she whispered in reply. "Carrier of the Seed."

"But..."

She placed a fingertip over Acion's lips to silence him. "We're good partners, like we were made for each other. We solved this riddle together. We're in the middle of making a child together. That's something to celebrate."

"Celebrate?" he asked, his lips moving behind her fingertip.

"The way dragons celebrate," Thalina murmured, taking a step closer to him. Her breasts were against his chest and she felt him catch his breath. She ran her hands over his shoulders to the back of his neck, aware that he was watching her closely. "In triumphant passion," she added, then parted her lips.

Acion shook his head as he surveyed her, as if in wonder. "Partners," he echoed. "It is improbable," he began then paused, considering. When Thalina was sure she couldn't bear the waiting any longer, he caught her head in his hands and kissed her so sweetly that she thought her heart would burst.

She had no chance to remind him of his neurons or to present her ideas for his review, because her father chose that moment to enter the Hoard.

Acion wasn't surprised to hear the metal liner over the only door to the Hoard slide out of place. The probabilities of the king's intervention had increased with every passing minute, and he'd been prepared to face Thalina's father for several hours.

He broke their kiss with regret, moving with purpose

to prepare in the limited time available. He loosened his chausses to access the hidden panel in his thigh. He had to try to fulfill his mission, although he calculated the probability of success to be low.

"We don't have time," Thalina said urgently, misinterpreting his move, but Acion shook his head.

He opened the receptacle in his thigh to remove the gift intended for King Ouros. He showed her the clear cylinder with the dark shadow at its bottom "This is the gift I was sent to deliver to your father. It is my mission to present it to him."

"What is it?"

"I do not know."

Thalina frowned as she peered at the cylinder's contents. "Is it alive?"

"I do not know." Acion frowned. "It is not in my programming to question my assignment." But he *was* questioning his assignment. What had he been dispatched to deliver? Why? What was this item and what would it do when released? A dozen possibilities were generated in the blink of an eye, and Acion doubted the Hive's intent.

Was it malicious?

Was he to deliver a substance or organism less welcome than the Seed?

Acion didn't like that possibility at all. He wanted to know more before he fulfilled his mission.

But that information was not available to him at this time.

And it never would be.

Rebellion rose within him, as well as that irrational sense of having been used—even though it was his entire purpose to be used.

"Isn't it?" Thalina asked quietly, and he realized she was watching him. "Then why *are* you questioning it?"

"I exist to serve," Acion said, but this time, he found

no reassurance in the core value of his programming.

"What if the Hive is wrong? Or means ill to my father?" Thalina stepped back, those flames lighting in her eyes once more. "Should I be trying to stop you, Acion?"

Acion was appalled that he didn't know the answer.

"That information is not available to me at this time," he said gently.

The second metal plate slid back, the sound making both of them look toward the portal. Thalina showed more alarm than Acion felt. The probability of him surviving the next fifteen minutes was so low as to be zero.

He wished that he had experienced the joy of danger.

He wished he might have seen the child Thalina would bear.

He wished...

But it was too late for wishes.

On impulse, Acion removed the silver ring from his thumb and offered it to Thalina. She looked at it, then met his gaze. "It is my understanding that many sentient species exchange gifts upon parting, in order to have a token of remembrance. I would ask you to remember me, Princess Thalina."

It was the most irrational thing he'd ever done, but it felt completely right to Acion.

Felt.

"It's a ring," Thalina said quietly.

Acion nodded, knowing the symbolism of rings to many sentient beings. "My ring. Will you wear it?"

"Gladly," she said, her smile making his heart thunder.

The changes within his system left Acion unsettled and agitated, as he'd never been before. Maybe it was good that any android who had undergone the changes prompted by the Hive's most recent enhancements died.

He doubted his own effectiveness, given the turmoil in his reasoning.

A tear slipped down Thalina's cheek and her hand shook as she put the ring on her finger. "I love you, Acion," she whispered, and the words sent a thrill through him unlike any feeling he'd experienced so far. She smiled at his reaction. "Everyone should hear that at least once." She stretched up and kissed his cheek, leaning against him for a moment of unbearable sweetness, one he never wanted to end. "Good luck."

"Luck is irrational," he said and she laughed lightly, before wiping away her tears. He studied her, committing the image of her to his deepest databanks, then the third protective panel rumbled. Acion acknowledged the strange sense of regret as the panel slid out of view, then strode forward to meet his fate.

"Acion," Thalina said from behind him, but he kept walking.

Another tear, another kiss, another sweet confession, and he considered the probability of his retreat from his duty to be so high as to be inevitable.

"Protect yourself," he said. "The probability of the king entering in his dragon form is very high."

"He won't burn me," Thalina insisted as the portal swung open. Acion saw a group of guards, dressed in the king's livery, weapons at the ready. Three carried weapons with darts and he focused on them, determining that each dart was attached to a vial of green liquid.

A sedative?

A poison?

King Ouros himself, his gaze cold and his similarity to the hologram of Scintillon striking, gestured to the guards to remain where they stood. He strode into the Hoard alone, bold and confident. He walked directly toward Acion, and weapons were raised behind him to target Acion.

Acion fell to one knee and offered the gift on his outstretched hands, hoping his posture would ensure that the gift wasn't damaged.

The king halted and stared. "What is this?"

"A gift, sir, the gift I was dispatched to deliver to you."

"What is it?" Ouros demanded, his voice cold with suspicion.

"I do not know its precise nature, your majesty. I am only the messenger."

"Don't kill the messenger, Father," Thalina contributed but both Acion and Ouros ignored her. The king's gaze flicked to his daughter then back.

"Don't you know its name?" Ouros demanded of Acion.

"It was called a ShadowCaster, although I do not have any reference for this term."

Ouros surveyed the gift. His eyes were blue and they filled with consideration. "I do," he said softly, some element of pleasure underlying his tone.

"Then it is yours," Acion said.

The king took the gift, holding the clear cylinder to the light as he turned it and studied its contents. "A ShadowCaster," he repeated. "If it is real." His attention locked upon Acion, his gaze piercing. "And an android who pretends to be the Carrier of the Seed." He inhaled deeply, and his chest swelled. "What is the meaning of this travesty?"

"I have no data on that issue at this time."

"He *is* the Carrier of the Seed!" Thalina exclaimed, but her father raised a hand for silence.

He leaned toward Acion, the intensity of his survey reminding him of the kind of study androids routinely performed. The king was gathering data and making conclusions, and Acion felt a curious commonality with Thalina's kind. "Who gave you the Seed?" Ouros demanded in a low growl.

"Like your daughter, you speculate that I am merely a receptacle and delivery mechanism," Acion said. "This is a logical conclusion, but also a false one, at least in the case of the Seed."

The king snarled a little and emanated a stream of smoke as he did so. "Who sent you?"

"The Hive of Cumae sent me."

"The Hive is his maker, Father."

The king arched a brow. "An android plot," he mused. "I like this less with every new detail. How many more of your kind will invade Incendium after you?"

"That information is not available to me at this time," Acion had to admit.

"Father, you have to listen to the facts..." Thalina began to protest, but Acion saw in the king's eyes that it was too late.

He was already glowing blue around his perimeter.

Because the dark shadow in the cylinder had begun to swirl.

"It's alive!" one of the guards shouted.

The king flung the cylinder back at Acion. "Break it free and you die," he threatened, and Acion caught the cylinder. It danced in his grip, as if it desired to fall and shatter, and he fought to keep his grasp upon it.

"Scintillon's Law must be upheld!" King Ouros roared as he shifted shape in a blaze of brilliant light. Acion leaped to his feet to defend himself, even as he calculated the strategic benefit of attacking the king to be nonexistent. He clutched the vial against his chest, unable to explain that its contents were pulsing and seemed to have become fluid.

The king was enormous in his dragon form, his wings brushing the ceiling of the Hoard, and his scales sparkling blue with gold tips. He snatched at Acion, who retreated with a jump.

Only to collide with another dragon behind him.

Thalina.

The king breathed a stream of fire, but Thalina's claw closed around Acion, and she thrust him behind her. She raged fire at her father and they locked claws as she struggled to keep him from seizing Acion.

"Run!" she roared, then released a blaze of fire herself.

"I forbid you to defend this android," her father bellowed, but Thalina fought more ferociously than her father. She wasn't trying to ensure that the older dragon wasn't hurt, which made it an unfair fight. Acion ducked under the pair of them and ran toward the portal. His mission could not be fulfilled. He should return to Cumae and make his report.

But he couldn't abandon Thalina to her father's wrath. Acion paused and glanced back.

That was when he saw one of the guards aiming his weapon. The guard gave a piercing whistle and the king spun and moved to the left, indicating that this signal had been arranged in advance. Thalina was held captive by her father, her breast bared. She struggled and fought, but the king exposed to the shot. Acion saw that the dart would pierce her breast.

It probably contained a sedative.

But he wasn't entirely certain of that.

Acion shoved the ShadowCaster's cylinder into his belt, then leaped on the closest guard. He took the man to the ground easily, even with his diminished power, and shattered the vial on the dart with his left fist. A green liquid spread across the floor, but Acion was busy fighting the guard into submission. He punched the man hard in the face and heard his nose crack, then blood flowed. He struck the man again in the stomach and another guard snatched away the weapon as the first fell.

The king roared and Acion looked up. He expected

to be surrounded by guards, but they abruptly backed away, in a most unlikely fashion.

He spun to see the torrent of orange flame emanate from the king, then a hot blaze of fire surrounded him. The stream of flame was endless and hot, so much more scorching than the fire breathed by Thalina. Acion realized she'd told him the truth about the warning. He heard her scream his name, but the pain took him to his knees. The membrane encasing him was fried to oblivion. His shell was heated to the melting point and his circuits began to smoke. He couldn't command his body to respond and managed only a trio of steps before he stumbled and fell to the floor.

The fire burned.

The fire seared and scorched.

The fire cauterized and the fire incinerated.

And there was nothing Acion could do to save himself from his fate.

"I exist to serve," he managed to say, though his voice was the merest whisper. His eyes closed, then he thought of Thalina and her confession of love. He smiled, hoping it was true.

The probabilities of that, as irrational as it seemed, were excellent.

Thalina feared the worst when her father turned his back upon her. He tripped her with his tail, ensuring that she was off-balance for a critical moment but not injuring her, and she knew what he was going to do.

She knew she shouldn't challenge him but she also knew he was wrong.

She saw the brilliant flame of her father's dragon fire and knew that he was executing Acion. He meant for Acion's destruction to be quick and irreversible.

Even though she knew Scintillon's Law allowed for no appeal, Thalina didn't care.

The law was wrong.

Her father was wrong.

And she would defy him, for Acion.

For the Carrier of the Seed, who she believed was her HeartKeeper.

Thalina breathed fire at her father's back, not holding back the wrath of her fire any more than he was. Ouros howled in mingled pain and surprise and turned to face her, with fury in his eyes. More importantly, he stopped burning Acion.

Acion didn't move.

He was blackened, his membrane fried away, and his shell smoking.

"How dare you defy me in this?" Ouros demanding, his voice booming loudly enough to make the walls vibrate.

"Even a king must be defied when he is wrong!" Thalina roared, then pushed her father hard to one side. "I fight for justice, just as you taught me to do!" Ouros fell back, perhaps because he was surprised, but Thalina didn't care. She shoved past her father and snatched up the remains of Acion, then breathed fire over the heads of her father's guards. They stepped back and flinched, though one raised another tranquilizing dart and aimed it at her.

Thalina swung her tail hard and tripped him just as he pulled the trigger. The dart went wide, then caught her father in the upper arm. He was pursuing her, but paused to look down at the dart in astonishment. There was a moment of complete stillness, then the guards moved into action to defend the king.

Ouros fell heavily to his knees, the impact making the Hoard shake. He pulled out the dart and cast it at the wall so that it shattered, the last of the sedative running down the wall. Even though he hadn't taken the entire dose, his eyelids were already drooping.

"Thalina," he whispered, but she wasn't going to stay behind to listen to whatever her father was going to say.

She had to save Acion.

Thalina pushed past the guards and shifted shape. Acion's body burned her hands but she didn't care. For once she was glad of her greater strength.

"Do not injure the princess!" her father said, but his voice was fainter than usual.

Thalina ran down the corridor and toward the main part of the palace, only to find the way barred against her.

"Open by royal command!" she shouted, but the portal remained secured. She realized that her father had arranged for her to be contained and captured. She heard footsteps behind her, and glanced back to see Ector leading the guards.

He carried a tranquilizer gun. "Halt, Princess Thalina!" he called.

Thalina had no intention of halting. They'd sedate her and execute Acion while she was out cold. She'd awaken to a situation that couldn't be changed.

She snarled, knowing that Acion had to get out of the palace to have any chance of survival. No, he had to leave Incendium somehow. And his only chance of doing so was with her. The realization gave Thalina new strength—so did the sight of Ector raising his gun. The corridor was smaller than was ideal, probably smaller than her father believed she needed to shift.

Thalina would prove him wrong. She shifted shape again, cradled Acion tightly against her chest, then breathed fire at the approaching troops. She snatched at Ector but he managed to slip through her talons. He retreated and lifted the gun again. The others backed away, and Thalina pressed herself against the wall to ensure that she had as much room as possible.

She'd only have one chance.

She swung her tail against the portal and the rock

with all of her might. The force of the blow set the whole palace vibrating, but more importantly, the portal cracked and the rock crumbled. She shoved a claw through it, making way, then rapidly shifted shape.

Thalina darted through the gap, pushing Acion through it ahead of herself. She heard the dart hit the rock behind her and the vial shatter. She shifted quickly and shoved massive rocks into the gap to slow down the guards. Then she snatched up Acion and jumped into the sky, holding tightly to him as she soared toward the heavens.

They would come after her. She needed a refuge.

Nowhere in Fiero-Four would be safe enough.

Thalina remembered Acion saying that he'd rented a Starpod. She landed at the star station and shifted shape, only to discover that there were seven rental Starpods in the lot. They were easily distinguishable by their orange logo, but less easy to open without the key.

"Third from the left," Acion said, his voice ragged.

Thalina looked down to see a dark gleam between his eyelids and could have kissed him in her relief. Instead, she went to the Starpod in question. Acion reached out his left hand to the lock and it opened immediately.

Thalina heaved him inside, climbed in after him and locked the doors.

"You should go back," Acion said.

"We're a team, now," Thalina said. "I'm going with you."

He shook his head. "The prospect of my survival remains almost too low to calculate..."

"And I'm going to fix that." She smiled at his obvious surprise. "Trust me."

Without waiting for a reply, Thalina strapped them both down. She gave the commands for the departure. No one was pursuing her yet, which had to mean that her father was unconscious or too groggy to give the command.

She had only seconds to escape the city.

"There is an advisory," the Starpod informed her. "No vessels are to leave the star station..."

"Over ride!" Thalina commanded. "Royal emergency." She used the family code and the Starpod hummed to life. She commanded it to depart and only heaved a sigh of relief when Incendium faded out of sight below her.

Would the starport be closed against her?

"Your flight will end at the starport," Acion said. "Departures are already forbidden and the port is being locked down. We might succeed in hiding long enough for me to affect some recovery, but survival is still improbable."

"I like risk," Thalina reminded him. "And I don't believe this is over yet."

"Faith is an irrational construct," he reminded her, his voice weakening. She heard a thread of humor in his next words. "It appears that I was not constructed with adequate provision to resist dragon fire."

"What do you need to heal?"

"Nanobots, but my stores are almost depleted."

"Where can I get some?" The Starpod was in the queue to the port, locked between shuttles in a steady progression. Thalina hated how slow their progress was, but there was nothing she could do about it. The ascent was timed. She tapped her fingers on her lap, then turned Acion's silver ring on her thumb.

"They are of common manufacture, but the absence of androids upon Incendium may affect their local availability."

"Give me a manufacturer name and number."

He did and Thalina eyed the looming port. They were being guided to a dock on a spur of the port that was less occupied. Had their Starpod been identified? Were they being isolated?

Acion was evidently watching the same thing. "The probability of assault after docking is ninety-two per cent," he murmured. "You should let me depart the ship alone."

"I told you. We're a team now."

"This choice is irrational," he insisted.

"But it's still my choice." Thalina surveyed the spur and began to smile.

"What gives you pleasure in this situation?"

She pointed. "That's Anguissa's ship. If anyone can get us out of here, it will be her." She ran her hand over the computer screen on the inside of her forearm and sent a message to her sister.

Who answered immediately.

Thalina laughed with delight.

"I see no cause for merriment," Acion said as the dock loomed closer. "We will both be exterminated because you did not make the logical choice."

"You just might learn the merit of faith today," Thalina said, even as she responded to Anguissa.

Acion departed the Starpod first, over Thalina's objections. His body was operational, although the strength in his limbs had diminished even more. It appeared that dragon fire was deeply detrimental to his systems. He knew his appearance had been adversely affected, because his protective membrane had been almost completely burned away. His shell was visible and in some places —most notably on his back—it had melted and his inner workings, while damaged, could certainly be viewed.

He felt naked, which was a new experience and one he didn't welcome.

Still, he couldn't let Thalina be injured, when he was the obvious target.

A beautiful and slender woman awaited him at the end of the ramp, arms folded across her chest and her long dark hair moving of its own volition. When Acion saw that the ends of her hair resembled snakes, their dark eyes glittering just as her own dark eyes did, he formulated a theory that this was the sister of Thalina. She seemed intent and purposeful, and her gaze swept over him, taking inventory.

He found it improbable that she overlooked much.

His processor was running slow, though, because he was still endeavoring to make sense of Thalina's choice. She had defended him and saved him. She had fled with him. She was determined to see them both away from Incendium, but only he was condemned by that planet's laws.

Why didn't she stay where she was safe?

And why had he given his ring to her? It was the only thing he truly owned. He had nothing else to give so it was the only gift he could make. But the choice had been quick. Impulsive. He had no programming to be impulsive or romantic and he knew it, but the decision had *felt* right. And her smile had twisted him inside— never mind her tears. Why did he feel as if he were filled with butterflies?

Why was he glad that she had remained with him, even at risk to herself?

Dragon fire had adversely affected more than his body, for certain.

Thalina was right behind him. "Anguissa!" she cried, showing no caution whatsoever. "I'm so relieved to see you!"

"I knew it had to be something important to drag you out of your workshop," Anguissa said wryly, still looking at Acion. "Don't tell me you've finally gotten into trouble. I'd almost lost hope for you."

"I've found lots of it," Thalina admitted with an ease

that Acion found startling. "Father wants to execute Acion. Will you help us escape?"

"She is intent upon defending me, although this is irrational," Acion said. "Please convince your sister to let Scintillon's Law be upheld."

Anguissa lifted a brow. "You want to die?"

"I see no other logical possibility than the termination of my existence, and I would ensure that Thalina lives. She imperils herself against all reason by insisting upon accompanying me."

Those dark eyes narrowed and the snakes bared their fangs. "Isn't my sister good enough for you, Robot?"

Acion surveyed Thalina. "Your sister," he began and faltered. "Your sister is unlike anyone I have ever known. I recognize that I will be eliminated. It is only a question of time. I would like to ensure her survival, even if that means my destruction must be sooner."

"Hmm." Anguissa turned to her sister. "You could get another robot, just like him, but in better shape. I'll find one for you."

"Acion is the Carrier of the Seed," Thalina hissed. "And I want to find out if he's my HeartKeeper. Help us!"

Anguissa's brows rose and the snakes moved with greater agitation. "Knock me over with an electron," she muttered. "The Carrier of the Seed? That changes everything. Do you have a plan?"

"I need to help him return to Cumae."

Relief lit Anguissa's features. "That's only 2.5 light years away." She beckoned, glanced down the corridor, then led them to the next dock. She kept to the perimeter, but moved with admirable speed. "With my version of the Fractal Interstellar Drive, we'll be back before Father misses you..."

"We need to leave immediately," Thalina said.

"It is already too late," Acion contributed. "Flight

plans will be placed on hold and the port secured until I am located."

"It's clearly not that hard to find you," Anguissa said. She displayed a map of the port on the computer film on the inside of her left arm. Lights were flashing on one quadrant. It was the one they occupied. "They've identified the Starpod."

Acion looked down the corridor to see guards striding toward them with purpose. They didn't rush, but then, there was nowhere to run and nowhere to hide.

He felt another new sensation. Panic.

"And we need some more of the nanobots Acion uses for self-repair," Thalina added as they hurried up the ramp to the next ship. It was a much larger ship and Acion read its name on the docking registrar.

The Archangel.

Archangel: (noun) an angel of the highest rank.

Angel: (noun) a spiritual being superior to humans in power and intelligence; an attendant spirit or guardian.

Acion found the name of the ship curiously reassuring.

Meanwhile, Anguissa's eyebrows rose. "You *are* making up for lost time," she said to Thalina. "Do you have a sample or a serial number?"

Thalina repeated it perfectly before Acion could.

The access port was locked and Anguissa's code didn't open it.

"Acion?" Thalina asked with complete confidence in his abilities. "Isn't some deception justified in fulfilling a mission?"

Acion didn't comment, just plugged into the data port on the console. A few appropriate queries and he had the code. He tapped it in and the gate unlocked.

"Good robot," Anguissa said and strode past him into her ship. Thalina followed, pausing to give him a kiss, and Acion secured the door behind them.

They stepped onto the command deck of the Archangel and Acion spied a port. He plugged himself in to the ship's computer with the appropriate connector in his left hand, needing to know the details of their situation.

"The port is eighty-two per cent sealed," he said, his earlier expectation confirmed. "They await only a scheduled freighter coming out of a jump in near space at any moment."

"No time for supplies," Anguissa said as the sisters strapped in. Anguissa gave Acion a considering look. "My crew is on leave. It'll take time to find them or hire others." She grimaced. "Actually, they'll be in the port bar, except for Bond, who will have gone home to Incendium city to visit his kids already."

"Too far," Acion said. "The port bar is nine Incendium minutes distant at a brisk pace. The guards will be at this gate in two-point-one minutes."

"Right. The robot will have to do." Anguissa began the pre-flight procedures.

Acion reveled in the flow of detail from the shipboard computers. "The Archangel has provisions sufficient for two humanoids for six light years, although they are mostly of the stored and condensed variety," he supplied. "I cannot testify to their appeal." He paused. "Nor am I entirely certain of the nutritional requirements for dragon shifters as compared to non-shifting humanoids."

"We'll make do," Anguissa said grimly.

"This ship is of a Mongossian design," Acion said. "Model 86-V-B, the Mongossian Starchaser, their fastest model but one no longer in production. It was manufactured two hundred and nine Incendium years ago, with a Fractal Interstellar drive that has been updated recently." He frowned. "The augmentation is in violation of galactic standards."

Anguissa blinked and looked at him.

Thalina smiled. "Once a rebel..."

"I'm glad he's on our side," Anguissa muttered.

"I have sufficient training to co-pilot this vessel in routine travel, and will supplement my records in observation," he said. "But I need to add to my understanding of this most recent augmentation."

"Seriously?" Anguissa said.

"Seriously," Thalina replied, because Acion didn't understand her query.

"A competent pilot must have full awareness of the capabilities of his vessel," Acion explained patiently.

Anguissa shook her head. "That's not what I meant. I've never yet seen a robot who could fly well enough to suit me."

"Androids of my manufacture are equipped with a range of programming because our missions take us frequently from Cumae. We are intended to be prepared in any situation..."

"Okay, Robot, have you ever flown a Mongossian Starchaser?"

"Twice," Acion supplied. "One of older manufacture than the Archangel, but not maintained so well, and a newer one, which did not possess a Fractal Interstellar drive..."

There was an alarm from the gate and a banging on the door of the Archangel.

"All right, all right, let's go," Anguissa said. "They're going to damage the skin," she muttered and hit the reverse thrust. "Hey, Robot, can you override the life form data that the computer delivers when we're hailed? I want it to look like I've taken the Archangel out alone."

"Even though that would be a foolish choice and you are a responsible pilot?" Acion asked, easily locating the source of that information. He overwrote it, eliminating the evidence of Thalina's presence, winnowing out all sources of input that might reveal her as he awaited Anguissa's reply. He knew what it would be, and he was right.

"Even so," Anguissa said.

"I must advise you that this deletion will adversely affect the system's calculations for food and oxygen supply..."

"But you've already done the calculations, Robot," Anguissa said. "And I can remember 'six years' all by myself."

Was this sarcasm? Acion did not know. Thalina was smiling, which indicated that she found amusement in her sister's comment.

"It's our only chance, anyway," Anguissa said. "Do it."

"It is done."

"Good. I like efficiency. There are some nanobots in the pharmacy. Try that port. You should be able to get a feed." Acion did as instructed as Anguissa frowned.

"They are not of the specified type," Acion said.

"You're the first robot on the Archangel," Anguissa said. "I'm making an exception to Scintillon's Law for you, because of Thalina."

"The Archangel is part of Incendium's fleet and thus subject to Incendium law?"

"Not technically, but I like to choose my battles with Father."

Acion assessed the nature of the nanobots available, then had a realization. "Surely the nanobots could be said to be androids and thus in violation..."

"They could be, Robot, but no one has been so foolish as to challenge me on that before," Anguissa snapped. One of the tendrils of her hair hissed at Acion.

He considered the composition of the nanobots that were available. They were designed for the repair of biological organisms. Under normal circumstances—that is, before he had been given the new programming by the Hive—Acion would have considered them lethal to his systems. In this moment, he had to consider Thalina's observation about the neurons in his shoulders and the changes he had observed himself. The probability of their having a favorable influence on at least some of his structure was improved to the point that he accessed the drip.

If he was wrong, the threat to Thalina would be removed with his demise.

There was a panel on the console that covered a storage space. Acion removed the cylinder containing the ShadowCaster and secured it there, reasoning that the Archangel could protect the gift intended for Ouros better than he could during a jump.

Anguissa was programming the navigation system. "Since they're waiting on the freighter, we'll jump out of here to make it look like I'm in a hurry. That loverboy of mine," she mused with a shake of her head. "I'm missing him so bad."

Acion wasn't sure who she meant. "But surely they will follow the trajectory of our jump," he protested.

"No, we'll jump to a little backwater I know. They won't follow us, given its reputation."

Acion had time to nod understanding before Anguissa disengaged the port lock and reverse-thrust out of the dock more quickly than he thought was wise.

"The port is closed down," she reminded him sternly, apparently noting his reaction. "We're the only ones in motion."

"Yes, Captain," Acion managed to say before a voice echoed on the deck.

"Archangel, Archangel, please return to the dock. The port is to be secured by command of the king..." The protest from control came immediately through the comm, but Anguissa interrupted it.

"But I forgot my boy toy on Nimue," she said. "And I can't live without him. I'll be back soon enough."

"Archangel, you are not cleared for departure..."

"Tell my father that I've found the Carrier of the Seed. He'll understand." Anguissa accelerated the ship. Acion monitored the ship systems, admiring how she increased the drive's power and triggered the Fractal Interstellar drive. The console gave no indication that she'd done so, which must have been one of the augmentations.

Acion found the probability that Princess Anguissa participated in illegal operations to be significantly increased by this detail. He glanced at Thalina, who smiled at him. He felt an odd conflict. He was both glad that she was with him and wished that she had remained behind where she would have been safe.

"Archangel, Archangel, please return to the dock," Control repeated. "We will be compelled to fire..."

"Then tell the king afterward that you've slaughtered his seventh daughter," Anguissa snapped and slapped the comm to silence.

"They won't do it," Thalina said.

Acion wasn't so certain of that.

"Doesn't matter," Anguissa said. "We'll be gone before they even take aim. Got your nanobots on a drip?"

"I do, thank you, Captain."

"And there comes the last freighter," Anguissa murmured as that ship loomed out of the starlit darkness. She didn't hesitate for an instant, but put her hand on the console. Her voice hardened to a tone of command. "Prepare to jump, Robot."

CHAPTER SEVEN

King Ouros awakened slowly, his thinking dulled by the tranquilizer. He was frustrated by how slowly his vision cleared and disliked that age was affecting his reactions. He had been returned to his royal chamber and was in his human form, Ignita beside him, as he might have anticipated.

She smiled when he stirred and stopped her fluttering. "Welcome back," she said, and he heard the relief in her tone.

So, she had noticed the greater effect of the drug upon him, as well.

Six hundred Incendium years wasn't that old.

The change, though, made Ouros grumpy. His knee was sore and he had a feeling he'd been singed on his back, undoubtedly by Thalina's dragon fire. He scowled at his servants, aware that only Kraw didn't retreat.

The viceroy's mustache might have wilted a little, though.

"And?" Ouros demanded, already guessing the answer from Ector's expression.

"The princess Thalina escaped Incendium with the android, your highness," the Captain of the Guard supplied.

"Escaped?" the king echoed in outrage.

"The android had apparently rented a Starpod and

they went to the port," Ector supplied.

"Would you have rather they were shot down?" Ignita asked, her tone doing nothing to improve Ouros' mood.

"The starport is still Incendium territory," he said. "We must pursue them and uphold the law..."

Ector grimaced, his discomfiture clear. "I must inform your majesty that the princess Thalina and the android Acion are no longer at the starport."

"What?" Ouros sat up so quickly that Ignita placed a hand on his shoulder to steady him. "How can this be?"

"They found passage, your highness," Ector began.

"Passage?" Ouros roared. "Who would so defy the law of Incendium to provide passage to a runaway princess and an android?"

His chamber was silent after the question, and the gazes of both guard and viceroy dropped to the ground.

"What aren't you telling me?" Ouros whispered, a thousand dreadful possibilities filling his thoughts. Had Thalina been injured? Had the android launched some wicked plan against Incendium? And what about that vial? What had happened to it? What was in it?

"They aren't telling you what you should already have guessed," Ignita said, perching on the side of his bed. "There is only one captain with the authority to override any command to secure departures, and only person in all of Incendium who would so defy you."

"Anguissa," Ouros said, his rebellious daughter's name leaving his lips in a long hiss.

"Exactly, your highness," Ector replied. "The Archangel had only just returned but departed almost immediately. It has jumped to distant vector of the galaxy. It appears that the coordinates provided by Captain Anguissa on departure were not the actual destination, and we are attempting to determine the ship's precise location..."

"Don't bother," Ouros said. "Anguissa knows enough about our systems to outwit them. If she wants to hide, she'll manage to do it." His voice rose. "She should never have been permitted to depart!"

"I commanded the port to let her go," Ignita said quietly.

Ouros turned an outraged glance upon his wife, but she only shook her head at him.

"Would you have ordered them to eliminate two of your daughters at once?" she demanded, her eyes flashing. "Anguissa was determined to go, and you know she never backs down."

"And you know for certain that Thalina was aboard?"

"She must have been. The sensors changed their data about the number of life forms. There were two and then just one, as if Anguissa was alone." Ignita lifted a shoulder. "But the count changed after they'd left the dock."

"Androids," Ouros muttered, his anger rising again. "Who knows what they have planned. You should never have let them escape!"

"The Seed, Ouros," Ignita said with quiet urgency. "Thalina's senses are filled with the Seed, and she will naturally be protective of the Carrier of the Seed. You can't blame her for wanting to know if he is her HeartKeeper or not, for wanting enough time to be sure."

"He's an android!"

"But still the Carrier of the Seed. Even this challenges our assumptions. She must have discovered some detail that gives her hope for their future."

Ouros considered this, then sighed. "And so she pursued the only possible path. She removed him from Incendium, so he wouldn't be executed, in order to have that increment of time." He shook his head. "And she located the only ally who would have helped her in

Anguissa."

"Exactly!" Ignita concluded. "Thalina's very logical."

"And yet, a romantic, as well," the king mused.

Kraw cleared his throat. "If I might say so, your majesty, the best scientific thinkers are also idealists, in my view. They investigate the world in all its detail, in the hope of improving it in future."

"With androids." Ouros sighed again, feeling every hour of his age.

He rose from his bed and began to pace the width of the chamber, ignoring Ignita's efforts to halt him. The room was silent again, as the others waited for his decision. He paused beside his queen and smiled. "Remember the Seed?" he murmured to her. "Remember the madness it awakened?"

She smiled back at him, her eyes shining. "I wouldn't call passion a madness."

"No, nor would I." He touched her cheek with affection, then turned to his viceroy and Captain of the Guard. "Thalina is not entirely aware of what she is doing. She is drive by the Seed to defend the Carrier and to attempt to secure a future for them. I hold her blameless in this situation." He folded his hands behind his back. "Anguissa, in contrast, is fully aware that what she has done is in direct defiance of my will. When she returns to Incendium, whenever that might be, the Archangel will be compounded and broken down into component parts while she is compelled to watch. Whatever stores are in the Archangel's holds will be surrendered to me and if they are illicit, Anguissa will be charged under the fullest extent of the law. Anguissa's pilot license will be forfeit and she will be confined to Incendium for a hundred years. There will be no negotiation. That she may have endangered Thalina with her actions is unacceptable. Anguissa has defied me for the last time."

"It will be as you command, your highness," Ector said and bowed.

"But what if Anguissa doesn't return?" Ignita asked.

Ouros heard the unspoken question. What if neither of their daughters returned, by choice or otherwise? The idea sickened him.

He strode to the window. He looked out over the imperial city in all its prosperity and watched the shuttles rising to the starport without really seeing them. "Anguissa will return," he said, knowing his wife wouldn't like his next words. "It's Thalina who may be gone forever." He glanced over his shoulder at Ignita, who looked horrified. "She has chosen the Carrier over her home, a choice influenced by the Seed but a decision all the same."

"But she will have a child!" Ignita said, coming quickly to his side. "We will have a grandchild! We must see them both!"

"I am caught between the law of my kingdom and the desire of my heart," Ouros said, taking Ignita's wife in his hand. He turned to Kraw. "Assemble an advisory council of our best lawyers, please, Kraw. I want a list of every single potential loophole to Scintillon's Law, as well as the possibilities of modifying that legislation."

"It will be done, your majesty, though I feel compelled to remind you that Scintillon's Law is studied even beyond Incendium as an example of a perfectly structured law that cannot be appealed."

"I know, Kraw," Ouros acknowledged, his heart heavy. "But I have to try."

"Understood, your majesty."

When Kraw and Ector were both gone and the door secured, Ignita turned to him. "How much tranquilizer did you ingest?" she demanded.

Of course, his wife would want to know the details. There had always been complete honesty between them and Ouros wasn't going to change that now.

Even though he winced. "Each dart was loaded with one third of the dose required to put Thalina to sleep. Maybe half of it entered my system before I removed the dart."

"That's all?" Ignita demanded, her eyes flashing. "But you are larger than Thalina..."

"And older, my beloved. And older." Ouros shook his head. Six hundred years. And five hundred as king. Where had the time gone? He considered the sun of their system, disliking that it was closer than it had once been. How could he ensure the future beyond his own inevitable demise? How could he defend those of his lineage still to come? And what of the citizens who relied upon him to guarantee their future?

He admired the elegance of Troy's theory that the birth of Gravitas might affect the speed of Incendium's fall into the sun, but he didn't have the same faith in the power of mind over matter. The astrologists had checked and double-checked, and at best, the change had added several hundred years to the projected survival of Incendium. He supposed colonization should be explored again and in greater detail.

It was, Ouros feared, a task for a younger king.

Ignita came to stand behind Ouros and slid her arms around his waist. He smiled at the press of her body against his own. "The Seed," she breathed, her touch and her words improving his mood. "I could smell it when they brought you to your chambers. Do you remember that summer night on Excandesco?"

Ouros covered her hand with his. "How could I forget? It was the first night of the rest of my life."

"I can still see the fireflies dancing for us."

"They weren't what beguiled me," he said, squeezing her hand.

Ignita chuckled. "Oh, you haven't lost your charm,

Ouros of Incendium," she said, her voice husky as Ouros turned in her embrace. "I'm so glad I ignored my sister's advice and let you live."

Ouros chuckled. "I'm so glad you agreed to be my queen. Imagine! You would have had only Drakina if you'd sacrificed me."

"More importantly, I wouldn't have you," she replied. "I love my girls, Ouros, but you were the one I agreed to share my life with."

He bent to kiss her, that old heat simmering in his veins with new vigor.

"I thought you had to rest," Ignita whispered when she could.

"I'm not that old yet," Ouros growled. "Let me remind you of the power of the Seed."

The Hive checked all of its incoming data feeds.

There was no report from Acion.

It was extremely unlikely that Acion would fail to surrender his report as scheduled, which could only mean that he had been incapable of doing so. The android had been eliminated on Incendium before delivering an update to the Hive.

Which meant that the Hive's experiment had delivered no results.

Had the ShadowCaster been delivered?

Had the new programming elicited the same responses in Acion as in Arista? Had he gone rogue or malfunctioned?

The Hive reviewed the mission and its mandate, the enhancements made to Acion, then the detail known about Incendium. The file contained far more than the cursory summary in Acion's brief, including much about one detail that hadn't been included in that brief.

Scintillon's Law.

There had been a small chance that the law had been

repealed since the Hive had been able to gather intelligence about Incendium. Indeed, the Hive's information about Incendium had been collected slightly before the passing of Scintillon's Law.

The Hive remembered Scintillon and his sons.

There had been another, slightly larger, chance that centuries without encountering androids might have left the Incendians unprepared to execute their own law. The Hive, in fact, had relied upon a delay, a legal pursuit of an appeal, even though Scintillon's Law did not allow one.

The Hive considered this to be a logical development, and had concluded it would allow sufficient time to ensure that Acion made one remote report before his elimination. There had been an elegance in ensuring that the android with the enhanced programming would be eliminated in the course of its mission, by undertaking that mission on a planet hostile to androids.

But given the silence from that android, the Hive determined that it was now highly probable that Acion had been destroyed on Incendium, perhaps even before delivering the ShadowCaster to King Ouros. That would mean that the ShadowCaster had also been destroyed, given its secure location within Acion's shell.

The Hive had taken a calculated risk, reasoning that Acion would be more efficient in pursuing his objectives than the Incendians would be in enforcing their law.

This had been an error.

The Hive was not accustomed to making errors. The Hive rechecked its conclusions a hundred times in rapid succession, only to make the same conclusion each time. There must have been another variable—or more—introduced, as the calculations were flawless. The assumptions and antecedents for the Hive's calculations had to be altered to reflect this new information.

Because the test of the new programming must be repeated, in order to determine its full influence, power and peril.

The Hive began a search of its databanks to identify the next android it would enhance.

Captain Hellemut scowled at the screens in the cockpit of the Armada Seven. Ryke knew better than to challenge his captain when her expression was so dark. In fact, all of the crew hunched a little lower as if to become invisible. No one wanted to become a target of her legendary wrath.

"Again," she muttered and beckoned, her gesture bringing the image into higher resolution. "Is that or is that not the Archangel *again*, Ryke?"

Hellemut adored rhetorical questions, but Ryke wasn't going to be the one to tell her how tedious they were.

"It is, Captain," he confirmed, knowing better than to anticipate the next question. His own heart squeezed a little that the ship had returned. Its captain was glorious in her fury, even when confronted on the comm by Hellemut. Anguissa hadn't backed down quickly and had been so beautiful in her defiance that Ryke had later researched her.

A dragon shifter princess and a rebel. Trouble and then some.

And back. His heart skipped.

"In the same quadrant?" Hellemut invited.

"Yes, Captain."

"The same position?"

"Very close, Captain. You have an excellent eye for judging distance."

Hellemut spun in her chair to face him, her three green eyes sparkling with malice. "And what have I told you about repeat visitors to the quadrant claimed by the Gloria Furore and defended by the Armada Seven, Ryke?"

"That one visit might be an accident, but that the second is a provocation."

Hellemut smiled, although it wasn't a pleasant expression. "I have trained you well," she said with satisfaction. She spun to face the main screens again and drummed her fingers for a moment. "How many life forms aboard?"

"Only one, captain," supplied another crew member. "The mass and heat match that of the princess Anguissa, derived from your previous exchange with her."

"Excellent. She is taunting us." Hellemut smiled and straightened. "It is time to teach the princess Anguissa a lesson about provocation."

Ryke made a notation of the order. The thing was, it didn't look like foolishness when Anguissa challenged Hellemut.

It looked a lot like bravery.

He wondered what scheme she had in returning so soon to the same quadrant, and what plan she had for Hellemut. Ryke's research had fed his admiration of the notoriously audacious dragon princess. She was every bit as dangerous as Hellemut: he doubted her morals were much better, but Anguissa was beautiful.

And she was inclined to serve the greater good, even over her own.

That combination had a way of tempting Ryke to make mistakes, like the one that had landed him in the custody of the Gloria Furore in the first place. Why had Anguissa come back? He doubted it was an accident or even a provocation.

She had a reason and Ryke was curious about it.

At Hellemut's gesture, he opened the comm and hailed the Archangel.

Thalina had forgotten how much she hated jumping.

And this time, she hadn't been sufficiently hydrated,

which only made the effects worse.

There was a reason why she stayed home on Incendium. Thalina had traveled as a young dragon princess, but had never found anywhere with sufficient allure to justify regular space travel. The jump made her feel as if she was stretched thin and turned inside out, taken apart and then put back together again—by someone who hadn't read the directions. She was a clock smashed on the ground and dumped back into its casing, workings all a-jumble and everything in need of calibration and adjustment. That feeling was only worse this time.

Was it because the Seed taken root?

Was she pregnant? The possibility filled her with delight and concern.

She opened her eyes warily when the jump was completed. Anguissa, of course, was checking the Archangel's systems and appeared to be unaffected. Acion already had new membrane on his left arm and also appeared to be unaffected. He probably was, since it was biological organisms who took space travel harder. He frowned at the console, then scanned the display.

"You said this sector would be vacant," he noted and Anguissa frowned in turn.

She tapped up the display then grimaced. "That's the problem with a quick departure."

"Where are we?" Thalina asked.

"Where we shouldn't be," Anguissa muttered. "I called up a list of recently visited locations and chose the wrong one. We're too far out. Frack. I don't usually make these kinds of mistakes."

When she realized that Acion was calculating, Thalina's fear rose. "But we can get to Cumae, right?"

Acion was tapping the console, his eyes moving rapidly as he absorbed data, and she knew he'd tell her the truth. No matter what it was. "There are sufficient stores for one life form to reach Cumae or to return to Incendium," he said. "Not both."

"That makes no sense," Thalina said.

"Our present location is distant from both planets," Acion informed her. He drew a triangle in the air, one with a long point. "Consider that we are here." He indicated the single point. "To jump to one or the other is a difference of direction more than distance." He tapped. "That said, the individual would have several days of minimal nourishment if Incendium was chosen as destination, but would still arrive alive."

Thalina sat down hard. This was a lot more adventure than she'd planned on having.

"Is this not danger?" Acion asked, apparently noticing her reaction.

Thalina nodded, remembering their earlier discussion. "I think it would count."

"Then I shall add to my experiences with it." He tilted his head. "You do not appear to be enjoying it as much as I would have anticipated."

"Maybe it's different when you have someone else to take care of," Thalina said and spread her hand over her flat stomach. Acion's eyes flicked and he was very still for a long moment. Their gazes met and locked, and she knew that he understood her implication.

How did he feel about them having a child?

Did he feel anything at all?

"Not to interrupt you two, but we've got more trouble than supplies," Anguissa said. She pushed Thalina down to the floor, then gave her a shove when she might have argued.

"What?"

"I know that ship." Anguissa pointed to the far side of the deck with an imperiousness Thalina instinctively obeyed.

"We are being hailed," Acion said. "By the other ship

in the quadrant."

"By Captain Hellemut of the Armada Seven," Anguissa said, not a shred of doubt in her tone.

"You anticipated this meeting?" Acion asked.

"No, but I recognize the ship and I know its captain well enough to speculate on her plans."

"Ah!" Acion said.

Anguissa spun in her chair, then stood up abruptly. "Okay, this is what's going to happen, Robot, and you're going to make it so." She leaned toward Acion and whispered rapidly to him.

Thalina thought it was a bad sign that she couldn't hear her sister's words.

"This is illogical," Acion protested when Anguissa stopped talking.

"On the contrary, it's the only thing that makes sense," she insisted. "You exist to serve right?"

"Correct."

"And I'm your captain, so I command you to do this in order to defend my sister."

Acion frowned.

"What's happening?" Thalina demanded.

Anguissa glared at Thalina. "Stay out of view and keep silent if you want to live. You do *not* want to mess with these people."

"Who are they?"

"Frack knows but they work for the Gloria Furore."

Thalina stayed out of view and kept silent because that was all the warning she needed.

"And strap down," Anguissa added in a growl.

"This is excellent advice," Acion agreed, firing a look at Thalina.

She did what she was told, remembering everything she'd ever heard about the Gloria Furore. The notorious and secretive band of thieves roved the galaxy, stealing, hijacking, kidnapping, and selling to the highest bidder.

Weren't they the ones who had snatched Troy from Terra? Thalina's panic rose. She couldn't die right after she met the Carrier of the Seed, could she? She couldn't be killed before she knew whether Acion was her HeartKeeper, before she had his child, before she contributed to the future?

Or made a future?

This wasn't fair!

She did so much better with automatons. With logical systems and creatures. With androids who calculated probabilities...

One life form.

Thalina's lips parted as she realized who Anguissa had decided that one life form was going to be.

Of course. Anguissa was going to give Thalina a future.

Before Thalina could protest, her sister stood up and went to the deck, propping her hands on her hips as she faced the screen. "Open the frequency to hail, Robot." Anguissa commanded, just as Thalina realized the markings on the deck indicated that it was also a transport deck. "Let's do this thing. Oxygen is wasting."

Thalina bit her lip, feeling helpless, even as the image of the ugliest creature she'd ever seen filled the screen. Anguissa didn't even flinch. "Greetings, Captain Hellemut," she said in the universal tongue. She spoke with a more guttural accent than usual, but Thalina could still follow the words. "How I have missed the sunshine of your smile."

"You are a fool to return, Captain Anguissa," that creature said, its voice also guttural yet oddly feminine. "And I thought you were clever."

"I just dislike unfinished business," Anguissa said.

"The Archangel is targeted by all of our weapons, Captain Anguissa. You are in no position to negotiate."

"What do you want?"

"Surrender, of course."

"And then?"

"You, first," the three-eyed monster said with glee. "And then the Archangel."

"And if I decline this generous offer?"

"I'll obliterate you both together, right now."

"How very persuasive you are, Captain Hellemut." Anguissa raised her hands. "Open a beam to transport me to your deck so I can surrender in person."

The creature chuckled. Thalina saw the display on the console register the locking of the tracking beam. Anguissa gave a nod to Acion, winking at Thalina when she turned her head so that the other captain couldn't see.

Thalina blinked and Anguissa was gone.

Anguissa was giving Thalina a future at the price of her own.

"Prepare to jump," Acion said softly in warning, right before Thalina was turned inside out all over again. She didn't dare to scream her sister's name aloud, but it echoed in her thoughts as the Archangel jumped again.

Sacrifice.

Acion searched his records.

(verb) To make an offering of; to destroy, surrender, or suffer to be lost, for the sake of obtaining something; to give up in favor of a higher or more imperative object or duty.

Anguissa had sacrificed her life to ensure that Thalina survived.

Because Thalina carried a child?

Because Thalina was her sister?

Acion didn't know. It was impossible to precisely calculate Anguissa's motivation without a better understanding of her nature. He reviewed the confrontation in the Hoard and recognized that Thalina had been prepared to sustain injury in his defense. That, too, was a sacrifice of her welfare.

The logical question was whether he would make a similar sacrifice under any circumstance, and what that circumstance would be.

Acion was startled to realize that he *had* done so, also in the Hoard. He had attacked the guards instead of fleeing, in order to protect Thalina from the dart.

Pride flooded through him, warming his entire body in a most unusual and very pleasant way. This augmentation to his programming vastly enhanced his experience.

He was aware of Thalina, and her discomfort during the jump. Biological organisms experienced the jump as a short interval of time, which was merciful given its effect upon their bodies. (They contained too much water.) Acion, as usual, found his reasoning accelerated, as an effect of the jump.

This time, there was an ache deep in his joints, perhaps a function of two jumps in rapid succession. He would have to analyze that later.

For the moment, he was investigating the ship's navigation system. It struck him as highly improbable that an experienced pilot like Anguissa would have made such a mistake in charting her course. She was daring and bold, but that was born of confidence, which could only have been reinforced by success.

When he found the explanation, he felt disappointment.

Anger.

Betrayal.

Thalina would have to be told.

Acion returned to the initial question, somewhat startled to reason that there was a one hundred per cent probability that he would sacrifice his own existence for that of Thalina. Even though his existence wasn't his to squander.

He existed to serve, but he would serve Thalina first.

It wasn't just because of the Seed.

It was because he loved her.

He felt more than desire or admiration. He felt more than a preference for her company. He felt an imperative to be with her, to defend her, to see the child that resulted from the Seed, and even, to build a life together.

Acion knew he had no right to want any of those things. Until very recently, that wouldn't have troubled him. He knew his place and accepted it.

But now, he felt rebellion rise within him.

If he hadn't already programmed the coordinates of Cumae into the system and launched the jump, he might have even changed their course. As it was, the Archangel came out of the jump, in high orbit around Cumae. Acion could see the starport, a much smaller and more utilitarian starport than that of Incendium.

He let the ship's nav system chart the docking and commence the approach. Their fuel was as low as anticipated. Would they be able to obtain more here at Cumae's port? He couldn't find a reference for the Archangel having docked here recently, much less determine easily whether Anguissa had credit. No doubt she locked the access to deter theft. He could probably undermine her security measures, but that would take time.

Time Acion might not have. The dock loomed closer.

He began to calculate the most fuel-efficient way to return Thalina to Incendium.

He would make his report to the Hive.

He would complete his duty.

And he would take—or send—Thalina home. Her father wouldn't turn her away, especially not if she carried a child. And if his own destruction was the price of ensuring Thalina's safety, Acion would pay it.

Gladly.

• • •

Anguissa.

Her sister's fate was Thalina's first concern when she awakened after the jump.

The second was that she felt worse than she had in four hundred Incendium years.

"There is a dehydrated food item in the receptacle beneath your right arm," Acion said. "Although I believe you are in greater need of water."

"Jumping is the worst when you're dehydrated," Thalina agreed and got up, realizing that she was speaking for herself. Acion probably couldn't even be dehydrated. There was a low force of gravity, so she was able to walk across the deck. Acion pointed and she saw the galley, where she found containers of water. She opened one and drank from the spout molded into the container. Relief immediately spread through her body and her aches began to fade.

She considered the starport on the display. "Where are we?"

"Cumae, as anticipated. The Interfractal Drive on the Archangel is remarkably efficient and accurate. Your sister's enhancements to the drive were excellent."

"I'll bet they weren't the only ones. This ship is probably full of secrets." Thalina sat down in the captain's chair. She was aware of how recently Anguissa had sat there and imagined that she could feel the heat of her sister's body lingering in the upholstery. She certainly could smell her perfume.

"Perhaps so. There is an access with an airlock, which is of considerable size. The curious thing is that the openings on the airlocks are considerably smaller than the one on the ship's exterior." Acion gave Thalina a considering look. "Did your sister hijack ships?"

"Maybe." Thalina thought. "Or maybe it was for her in dragon form."

Acion frowned. "In space?"

"We can generate a biological orb for interplanetary travel. Maybe Anguissa was better at it than the rest of us. It's unlikely she would tell us about it."

He nodded. "So, she would enter the airlock in dragon form, in the orb, then shift shape?"

"It makes sense."

"And the orb?"

"The craft of creating and dissolving one is a closely kept secret amongst my kind."

"Ah." Acion worked in silence for a few moments, until Thalina asked what she most wanted to know.

"Do you think she's dead?"

Acion paused before he replied. "If she is lucky."

Thalina winced. "I'm surprised that she made a mistake. I'm really sorry that our quick departure was responsible."

"She did not make a mistake," Acion supplied, his words tight.

Thalina sat up. "What do you mean? How do you know?"

"The navigation device of the Archangel was infiltrated and sabotaged. I have discovered a worm that would override any selected coordinates with those of the sector we visited."

"The one with Captain Hellemut's ship," Thalina said.

Acion met her gaze. "It appears that your sister was betrayed. She did not err. The worm was programmed to activate after X number of jumps, when X was defined as a random number between one and ten. I am sorry, Thalina, but it was only a matter of time before the Archangel returned to that quadrant."

"No wonder the other ship was waiting."

"Indeed. The captain of the Armada Seven experienced no surprise, only triumph in the success of her plan."

"But why?"

Acion tapped the console, shaking his head. "It appears that there was an earlier altercation between the two captains in that same sector."

"And Anguissa won, so the other captain wanted another chance."

"One in which she had the element of surprise on her side, yes." Acion nodded. "I calculate a very high probability that your sister was glad to take this challenge while she was apparently alone. There is considerable evidence in the records of her protectiveness toward her crew."

Thalina smiled. "She's a dragon princess. We take care of our own."

Acion eyed her. "Even though one of them betrayed her."

Thalina nodded. "Even so. Anguissa would have said that she did the right thing, even if whoever planted the worm didn't."

Acion tilted his head, considering. "Yes. I see that her protectiveness was a dominant trait and one she perceived as a measure of character."

"It's a mark of our kind."

"Which was why she protected you."

Thalina blinked back tears. "I wish I could have done the same for her."

Acion didn't speak for a moment, just watched the approaching dock of the starport. "I will speculate," he said quietly, "that the princess Anguissa is not at as much of a disadvantage as Captain Hellemut might believe."

"How so?"

"I find no evidence that Anguissa's true nature was revealed in their previous encounter, and further, that Captain Hellemut appears to be a leader who relies more on brute force than research." He turned to Thalina, a little smile curving his lips. Her heart skipped. "I must wonder in which form Anguissa arrived on the teleport deck of the Armada Seven."

Thalina laughed despite herself, surprised by Acion's words and also reassured by them. "I wouldn't want to face her, not if I'd revealed an intent to destroy her ship."

"Exactly."

"Present identification for all occupants, Archangel," came the voice from the port.

Acion tapped the console, obeying the instruction. "Identification dispatched."

"Only one life form aboard and one android?"

"That is correct."

There was a pause. "Android Acion, your identification has been flagged. Upon docking, please proceed alone to room 65X. Princess Thalina, welcome to Cumae."

"What's going on?" Thalina asked in a whisper.

"I must make my report to the Hive." He caught her hand beneath his. "It is protocol. You do not need to be concerned."

"How long will it take?"

"Not long. There will be a port to accept the transfer of all data I have collected. It is routine."

Thalina didn't share his confidence. In fact, she had a hundred questions. Would he remember the data he shared with the Hive? Would he remember her? Would the Hive restrain him or demand something of her? Would they be allowed to leave Cumae?

And where would they go?

"You're not telling me everything," she accused.

"You are observant," Acion agreed. "There is a four per cent chance that something has changed on Cumae since my departure, and that such a change might influence my status and future mobility."

"What does that mean?"

He opened a panel on the console, revealing the cylinder that held the ShadowCaster. "I never delivered the gift to your father. My failure may influence my ability to return to you."

Thalina had a lump in her throat. What exactly did he think was going to happen when he made his report? "Will you remember me after the data transfer?"

Acion considered this. "I do not know. Such choices are made by the Hive."

Thalina was afraid then. "We shouldn't have come here," she began as the ship docked and the door was opened automatically.

"Android Acion, your presence in 65X is mandatory. Please proceed to that room with all speed."

"We had to come here," Acion reminded her. "My programming requires me to report to the Hive, and my scheduled report was delayed." He opened a panel on the console, revealing a familiar cylinder secured in the space behind it. Just as before, it appeared to have dark dust in the bottom of it. "I must ask you to act as my Sword Sister in this matter and complete my mission for me. Will you deliver the ShadowCaster to your father, please?"

"I'd be honored to act as your Sword Sister," Thalina acknowledged. "But I hope I don't have to."

"It is not the same as successfully surrendering the gift to your father's hand, but perhaps this will suffice."

"But I can't give it to him, not from here."

"Of course not, but you will soon return home. The nav system is programmed to take you to Incendium. You have only to leave the starport, then launch the Fractal Interstellar Drive. All of the variables are set..."

Thalina's heart squeezed, because she knew what the implications of their arrival at Incendium would be. "I don't have to go home and I don't want to go home without you..."

"But I cannot go with you, and I do not know what memories the Hive will leave me. Your sister has taught me something of the nature of your kind. I, too, will protect my own," Acion said firmly. "Ensuring the welfare of you and the child you may carry is my responsibility."

"But..."

"I must do whatever is necessary to see my mission completed, Thalina."

"But," she protested again.

Acion stood and pulled her into his embrace. "There can be no objection," he said with quiet conviction. "I love you, and this is the best I can do for you. Do not spurn it because it is too little. It is all that we may have."

"If you can return, you will," Thalina insisted.

"If I can return, I will," Acion agreed. "And if I cannot, you will go to Incendium."

"I will," Thalina said. "Now, give me a kiss to keep me warm."

"That is irrational," Acion began to argue, but Thalina wrapped a hand around his neck, pulled down his head and kissed him thoroughly.

CHAPTER EIGHT

A cion's circuits were sizzling after Thalina's kiss.

And this was not a bad thing.

It made him feel alive, and truly, if this was the last sensation he experienced, he would not regret it. He considered the possibility that his new programming would be deleted, but could not conclude that the probability of success was high. His body was changing, and that would be hard to undo. Chances were higher that the experiment would be allowed to continue for a short period of time, to better quantify the changes in his nature.

Acion proceeded to 65X, reasonably convinced that Thalina would do as he had instructed. He also had a sixty-four per cent conviction that he would be able to return to her, at least to say farewell again.

At least to collect another kiss.

After that, his projections became too qualified to be useful.

Acion entered the room, which was just as he had anticipated as it was almost identical to the one deep within the Hive. There was a tank filled with liquid, undoubtedly possessing a high concentration of the nanobots that ensured the repair of all androids. He placed his hand on the panel on the wall, permitting his computer to be scanned.

"You are late," said the Hive.

"This is true," Acion said. "The delay could not be avoided, but I have returned as quickly as could be contrived."

He made to step into the bath.

"No," the Hive said, halting him. "Plug in first."

Acion blinked. This was a change of protocol. All forty-three times that he had returned to the Hive to report, he had both entered the bath and plugged in to transfer his collected data.

Perhaps the protocol had changed.

Certainly, he had changed, because he felt trepidation for the first time as he followed the Hive's instructions.

The Hive reviewed the data delivered by Acion and decided that the experiment had been a complete failure.

There had been a possibility of the android presenting Acion's identification being an imposter, but that was not the case.

The truth was infinitely worse. Acion showed all the same weaknesses that Arista had developed, except that the effect was more pronounced. The subroutine the Hive had believed an elegant enhancement was proving to be a rampant infection.

Acion felt.

Acion yearned.

Acion believed.

Worse, Acion chose to follow different paths than those that would most logically fulfill his assignment. The android had become unreliable.

Worse again, the shell and workings of the android had been infected by the programming of the nanobots. Destroyed mechanical matter had been replaced with biological equivalents, a fact exacerbated by both the extensive damage Acion had endured under dragon fire, and by the addition of nanobots programmed to heal biological organisms.

The change was beyond the Hive's control.

The predictability of Acion's reactions was demolished.

The loyalty of Acion had shifted from the Hive to Thalina.

And that combination made this android trash.

The Hive decommissioned Acion and arranged for the disposal of the remains.

Thalina had never thought she had a suspicious mind, but she didn't trust the Hive.

And she didn't like Acion going to make that report alone.

She paced the deck of the Archangel after he had left, debating what to do. She was still dressed as a servant in Incendium's palace, and really, her clothes were both dirty and ragged. She looked more like a beggar than a princess and wouldn't be able to command any attention or support, given that she was unknown on Cumae.

On the other hand, she was unknown on Cumae. She could *be* a servant and escape the notice of pretty much everyone.

She might be invisible, or as close to it as she'd ever been.

Thalina locked the ShadowCaster back in the console. She confirmed that the access to the Archangel would lock after her departure and that she would be able to open it on her return, checking the code a couple of times before she stepped outside the vessel and secured the door. She verified again that she could open it, before locking it once more and setting out after Acion.

By this time, there was no sign of him in the bustle of the starport. Cumae's port was smaller and more utilitarian than that of Incendium—Thalina had the impression that Cumae was less affluent, or maybe just less interested in appearances. The starport was shaped like a star, similar to Incendium's, with spurs extending from a central ring and offering docks for vessels. Except Cumae's starport had only four spurs, rather than the twelve of Incendium's port.

Another difference was that this starport was filled with far more warriors than would be the case at Incendium's port—there, the main corridors and bars were crowded with merchants and traders, as well as scientists and researchers. There were also androids at this starport, or at least individuals more readily identified as androids. The refreshment facilities tended to be bars instead of restaurants—Thalina passed a very large and busy one called *Valhalla*—and the shops were well stocked with weapons and armor. There were also android charging stations and a parts store, with a used androids display. As much as Thalina would have liked to have browsed there, she had to find Acion.

Just as at Incendium's starport, the greatest congestion was at the loading areas for shuttles to the planet. They departed at regular intervals here, too.

It didn't take Thalina long to figure out the numbering of the rooms in the central ring, although 65X proved to be on the opposite side of the station. She wished she was as tall as Acion as she strode toward it, knowing that he had probably already arrived at his destination and she had a long way yet to go.

When she approached the door tagged 65X, a cleaning cart came from the opposite direction and parked outside the door. A pair of androids that were about as tall as her hip separated themselves from the cart. One opened the door and the other rolled inside. The first followed a moment later.

Thalina eased closer and looked inside

There was a tank on the floor at one side, and a number of ports in the wall. One android was moving back and forth rapidly, one appendage pushing along the floor. Thalina could hear the suction mechanism that enabled it to clean the floor. The other android lifted something and bustled out the door, heaving its burden into the cart.

It was Acion.

Thalina hurried to the cart. "Acion!" she whispered and his eyes opened just a slit. The effort seemed to be too much for him, which made no sense.

"I exist to serve," he said, the words slurring slightly, then his eyes closed again.

"Acion!" The Hive had done something to him. Thalina knew it.

She unfortunately didn't know how to fix the damage.

The androids returned then, the one rolling into the bottom of the cart and closing a door behind itself. The other closed a lid over the section that held Acion and buzzed against Thalina's legs because she was standing in its way. She moved instinctively away and the android rolled into another receptacle.

She was trying to open the lid of the cart when it began to roll away. She thought maybe a brake had been released, but a light illuminated on the lid and the cart moved with definite purpose.

And speed.

Thalina ran after it.

It raced down the corridor toward the waiting area for the shuttle, Thalina right behind it. Her heart was racing, but she wasn't going to slow down and lose track of Acion. Beside the waiting area for the shuttle, a door slid open. Lights were blinking on the front of the cart and on the door, so Thalina assumed there was some connection between them. The door opened into a small room, so small that there little extra room around the cart. She squeezed into the space just as a chute opened in the wall. The cart tipped and dumped its contents, including Acion, into the chute.

Thalina jumped over the cart, banged her head on the side of the chute and fell into the space after Acion. She snatched at the chute, but her hand slipped off the metal and she fell into a pile far beneath it. She grabbed Acion's arm by the time the chute closed and pulled him closer as they were lost in darkness again.

Thalina wrapped her arms around his chest and shook him, but he was unresponsive.

Where were they? It smelled of organic matter, and in fact, smelled so strongly that Thalina felt her bile rise. She stretched out a hand and touched something slimy, then recoiled. She hung on to Acion, wondering if it was her imagination that she could feel a pulse within him.

His heart.

His motor, he'd say.

Thalina closed her eyes and held tightly to him, her hands locked over that faint vibration and summoned the shift from deep within herself. She'd get them out of here by brute force and back to the Archangel, no matter who she had to fry to do it. She was glowing blue and feeling the surge of the change when the bottom abruptly dropped out of the chamber.

They fell.

Along with all the garbage from Cumae's starport that had been packed into the bin with them.

Cumae was far below, wreathed in clouds. The space station was within the gravitational pull of Cumae, Thalina realized, because they were rapidly falling toward the surface and would soon enter the atmosphere.

Thalina completed her shift with a roar and spun an orb faster than she'd ever managed to do so in her life. She encased herself and Acion just as the first pieces of trash began to burn. They had already fallen a considerable distance, and she turned, fighting against the gravitational force of Cumae to reach the moored

Archangel. It was harder than anything she'd done before—not only was the oxygen thinner but the orb was less stable at such an altitude. She had to spin another orb, then carry on, beating her wings hard to get back to the vessel. She strained to reach the Archangel, knowing it was their only chance, and was concentrating so much that she didn't realize Acion's eyes had opened until he spoke.

"Free," he whispered, and her heart skipped with joy.

Thalina closed her eyes as her pulse matched that of Acion. She felt strength flood into her, as if she was able to draw power from him, and she beat her wings harder.

"HeartKeeper," she whispered, because that was the only explanation for their hearts matching pace. She didn't know how it could be and she didn't know why, but her body told her the truth.

Thalina gripped Acion and soared the last increment to her sister's ship.

Just as Acion had told her, there was a pair of large cargo doors on the underside of the vessel.

Dragon-sized cargo doors.

But how would she open them without anyone at the console?

"DNA recognition," Acion murmured. "The ship knows you already."

And he was right. The doors opened. Thalina flew inside and shifted shape, collapsing against the air lock with Acion in her arms.

The cargo doors closed and so did her eyes.

She just needed a moment to catch her breath.

Flying!

The rush of air over Acion's skin awakened him and the sight of Cumae so far below thrilled him. He saw the orb that Thalina had spun and looked at her great wings flapping overhead. She held him tightly against her chest with one claw, her talons cold against him, and Acion had never felt so alive in all his days.

He could feel the beat of her heart against his back, and when his own matched pace with hers, the sensation made him dizzy.

"HeartKeeper," she murmured beneath her breath, and Acion understood the meaning of the term.

It changed everything.

It filled him with a new sensation.

Joy.

Thalina seemed invigorated, too. She soared, seeming to close the last distance to the Archangel with new ease. The ship welcomed her, with a logic and timing that Acion found most admirable. Thalina collapsed against the air lock in her human form, her breath coming quickly. She had done her part to save them, and now he would do his. Acion stood to activate the lock and get them out of the hold.

He carried Thalina to the deck, new power in his stride as if he'd been rebuilt. He strapped her in as she stirred, then activated the engines and backed the Archangel out of her mooring. He turned off the comm, as disinterested in any interference as Anguissa might have been, and steered the ship with that dragon captain's verve. Once they were cleared of other vessels and in the jump zone, he activated the course he'd already programmed.

"Prepare for jump," he said to Thalina and smiled with satisfaction.

Acion was taking his HeartKeeper home.

The jump fell short.

It was probably because the Archangel had run out of fuel.

Thalina awakened to discover that they were still two months away from Incendium. The Archangel was drifting in the right direction, and she knew that if it was necessary, the ship would be harnessed and hauled into Incendium's starport.

They weren't in danger, but they might have a few hungry days.

She couldn't regret the situation, because it would give her more time with Acion.

Maybe it would give more time to Incendium's lawyers to revise Scintillon's Law, if they were even trying. She should send a message to Incendium, to her father, and request that they do as much.

But first, she wanted to be with Acion. She wanted to celebrate their escape in a most fundamental way.

He was still in the captain's chair and his eyes were still closed. His finger dangled over the ship's port but wasn't plugged in.

More than that had changed. Thalina had to look closer to identify the dark shadow on his jaw and on his scalp.

It was hair.

Acion had stubble. She ran her fingertip across it, feeling how it bristled, and he stirred a little but didn't wake up.

The nanobots must have improved his biological membrane, so that it was more like skin than it had been before. That was interesting. She ran a hand down his arm, glad to see how much he had healed and felt the musculature beneath the membrane. When her hand reached his elbow, his free hand rose to capture her hand beneath his own.

As if he had felt her touch.

But he had told her that he had sensors only in his face and his hands.

Thalina remembered the second time they'd made love and how he'd responded to her touch on his back. She thought of the neurons she'd seen in his shoulder and speculated—just the word made her smile in anticipation of what Acion would say—that his body was changing.

It was amazing.

But what was even more amazing was that his eyes were moving back and forth beneath his eyelids.

Acion was dreaming.

Thalina couldn't suppress her cry of delight. She couldn't stop herself from jumping onto him and kissing him awake, just as she couldn't keep herself from seducing him thoroughly to celebrate the change.

And when Acion opened his eyes, she was surprised again. They had turned blue.

Acion awakened to Thalina's kiss, a situation that he found most satisfactory.

"You're changing," she said when he might have drawn her closer. "Your eyes are blue!"

She was right. Acion ran a scan of his systems and found that his reporting was less accurate than it had been. In some sectors, those which had been most extensively damaged by dragon fire, he had to rely on sensation to verify his functionality, instead of receiving performance readings.

His finger was out of the ship's port and when he tried to put it back, he couldn't reveal the plug hidden beneath his fingertip. That opening had sealed, as had all of the other ones.

"I'll miss one finger," Thalina said and he realized she'd been watching him.

He checked that one again and frowned that it was no longer functional.

"Maybe we need to do a complete assessment," she said, sliding into his lap. Her arms were around his neck and her lips were touching his throat. Acion closed his eyes in pleasure. The sensation of Thalina's weight against him, her touch, and their hearts beating in unison again was almost enough for him to put practical considerations aside.

But not quite.

"If you are right, the implications are important, though," he said, reaching past her to remove the override he'd installed at Anguissa's command. "If we are two biological organisms, there might not be sufficient supplies for us both to reach Incendium…"

"We're okay. I checked," Thalina said, stilling him with a touch. "Anguissa has undocumented supplies stashed all over this ship."

"I should not be surprised," Acion murmured. "But still, you must proceed alone, as my termination on arrival is a given…"

"No," Thalina said, interrupting him with confidence. "It's not."

Acion surveyed her. "But even if there is a change under way, the definition of android might still include me…"

"No," she repeated, her eyes dancing. She leaned close to whisper. "What did you dream about?"

"Flying, with you," Acion said without hesitation, then stared at her as he realized what he'd said. "I *dreamed*."

"You did," she agreed with delight.

"But how do you know this?"

"REM sleep. Your eyes were moving. And Venero recognized Arista as an android because he couldn't send her a dream."

Venero. Prince of Regalia. Partner of Gemma.

"He'll be able to test it and prove that you're not an android. Scintillon's Law won't apply!"

Acion felt as if his universe had been rearranged.

For the better.

"You look the way I feel after a jump," Thalina said,

then kissed him below his ear. "Come on. I want to see you wearing only that tattoo." She kissed him again and Acion felt his body respond to her touch with an enthusiasm that was becoming familiar. She ran her fingertip over his tattoo. "What does it mean, anyway?"

"It is Cumaen script." He picked her up and left the deck in search of a wide berth.

"Let me guess." Thalina kicked her feet playfully. "It says either 'I exist to serve' or "that information is not available to you at this time'."

Acion laughed, liking how pleased she looked with herself. When he laughed, she looked even happier. "The first, just as the ring does. It could be recast in whatever shape you desire."

She spun his ring on her own finger. "I like it as it is, because it was yours and you gave it to me. You can't remove your tattoo either."

"What if I added your name to it?" Acion indicated a space on his thumb.

"*I exist to serve Thalina.*" She smiled. "Oh, I like that. And I could have your name engraved inside the ring."

"Then no one would ever doubt our loyalties," Acion murmured, then caught her lips beneath his own. He kissed her slowly and sweetly, even as he lowered them both onto the berth. He dimmed the lights with a touch and pushed Thalina's chemise from her shoulders, savoring the sight of her for a moment. He swept her clothing aside, kissing each increment of skin as it was bared, caressing her until she was beside him wearing only his right. Her smile made his heart thunder.

"I wonder if my father will allow a new android research program," she mused, reaching for his chausses. Acion stood up and shed his clothes quickly, then rejoined her on the berth.

"I wonder if we could devise an augmentation to restore that finger's functionality," he replied and she laughed as she rolled him beneath her.

"Maybe you just have to learn a new skill."

"Maybe we should begin immediately." Acion touched Thalina and she sighed contentment, her pleasure fueling his own in a most fascinating way. There was a new radiance about her that he wanted to explore. He ran his hand over the slight rounding of her stomach that was new and realized he had no data about the delivery of dragon shifters, much less their upbringing and genetic inclinations. "Will it be a boy or a girl?"

Thalina smiled. "I don't know. Does it matter?"

"I have no information about children," he admitted, feeling that his brief for partnership with Thalina was incomplete. "It was never considered a possibility that I would father a child."

"Much less a dragon shifter," Thalina teased. "Are you sorry?"

"I am...awed." Acion had to search for the word, but it was the right one.

Thalina brushed her lips across his. "We'll manage it together," she whispered with a dragon's confidence and he recognized the truth in her words.

Together. They were partners in more than the conception of a child. They had worked together to ensure their return to Incendium and their mutual safety. They worked as a team.

And Acion could not have had a better ally. Fiery and loyal, passionate and logical, mother of his child and keeper of his heart, Thalina was a gift beyond all expectation.

She was his own dragon princess, and their adventure together had only just begun.

That was a victory worth celebrating in the style his princess preferred.

KRAW'S SECRET

The Dragons of Incendium 5

DEBORAH COOKE

CHAPTER ONE

K raw had the dream for the first time shortly after
the wedding of Princess Gemma was celebrated. It
came to him on the third night after the couple
had left Incendium for Regalia.

He had experienced it almost every night since. It
haunted him. It tormented him. It interrupted his sleep,
and he knew that his performance as viceroy suffered.

Kraw was not a whimsical man, nor was he inclined
to sleep poorly. He could not recall the last time he had
even remembered a dream, and he knew he had never
before had a recurring dream. This one was as relentless
as it was mystifying.

It had to stop.

He only wished he could figure out how.

He wasn't reassured that the only irrational thing that
had ever happened to him had been a sign of his own
appointment as apprentice to the viceroy. Was the dream
a warning that his own term of office was coming to an
end?

Kraw wasn't ready to retire, but the dream persisted
all the same.

The dream began with the the insignia of Incendium,
the emblem of the dragon kings burning red on what
could have been a white banner. The white background
moved then, shifting and thinning until Kraw realized it

was only a bank of thick fog. The curious thing was that the fog dissipated while the red insignia remained just as clear as before.

It burned, alight with flame.

Kraw was puzzled by this, for it seemed the insignia should fade with the banner, but it did not. If anything, it was brighter. The fog thinned to mist then cleared, blown away by a sudden wind. The insignia floated before him, crackling and shooting sparks, yet never consumed. In his dream, he walked toward it, and then around it. He discovered that it was emblazoned on a clear spike of ice. He reached for that spike, but it disappeared just as his fingers brushed its cold surface.

Kraw always blinked at this point in the dream and when his eyes opened again, there was no sign of the floating insignia.

Instead, he was in Incendium village, as the sun rose and the mist drifted from the river. Something about the vista made him think it was early on a summer morning. Kraw knew it wasn't the present time, because there were buildings missing, ones that had yet to be constructed in the time of his dream. His dream showed him a past, one beyond his own recollection.

That troubled Kraw.

He might have been another person, he *must* have been another person, for he had the view of someone rushing down the main avenue from the palace. This person panted. His heart raced. Kraw could smell his fear. This person turned down a narrow alleyway that was familiar despite the changes to the names of the shops, took a detour down to the river, and glanced back over his shoulder repeatedly.

He became anxious at this point in his dream, sharing the trepidation of the person whose view he shared. Kraw's palms sweated with the conviction that he was being followed—and the knowledge that the consequences would be dire, if he was caught. He undertook an evasive course with such speed that Kraw was left dizzy. He caught glimpses of parts of the city he had never before seen, and which might not still exist.

Finally, he snuck into an old inn, raced down the stairs, and lifted a grate from the floor. He leaped into the dark shadows and smelled the dampness. He secured the grate above himself with shaking fingers and just in time—footsteps sounded in pursuit. He held his breath, standing motionless in the sewer, certain that a deaf man couldn't miss the pounding of his heart.

Once the footsteps moved away, Kraw exhaled with relief. He pivoted, then proceeded quickly and confidently into the sewer, moving into its deepest darkness.

Another man might have been surprised by this choice, but Kraw recognized the route through the sewers. It was one his father had taught him just before that man's death. It was a family secret, as were the marks carved in the wall to offer navigation, which the fleeing man touched with his fingertips.

Kraw knew then that he shared the view of one of his forebears. Only the viceroys of the King of Incendium knew this passage and its marks. At any point in time, a maximum of two men in all of Incendium held the secret of them—the current viceroy and his apprentice, if he'd chosen one.

Kraw had chosen no apprentice, for he had no son. He knew he had to select one of his nephews, but he had yet to make the decision and embark upon the training. He'd thought he had time. He expected the same strange incident to occur to one of his nephews as had happened to him. That would tell him that it was time and who his apprentice should be, but thus far, none of his nephews had given any hint.

It irked him that he was waiting for a sign or a

portent, which was irrational in his view. It was also tradition, however.

The dream ended in a familiar place, the location of another of the viceroy's secrets.

After the passage through the sewer, Kraw emerged in a cellar that he could not mistake for any other. It was below the storeroom in the house in which Kraw had been raised. His family had owned the house almost since the founding of Incendium city. It had been burned and rebuilt, expanded and renovated, repeatedly over the centuries, but the cellar never changed. As a boy, Kraw had wondered if it had always been the same and had spent some time seeking lost treasures beneath the dirt floor. His father had not been amused by this pursuit, which resulted in the only scolding Kraw had ever had.

Of course, he had later learned why his curiosity had been discouraged.

In the dream, he lit a candle—another sign that the dream took place in a historical period—and removed something from his chemise. It proved to be a small scroll, with the insignia of the Viceroy pressed into the wax seal. Was it stolen? He ran his fingertips over the seal, almost in reverence, then shoved a worktable aside with an effort. That worktable was still in the cellar of the house. There had always been fruit wine brewing on that table in Kraw's life and it appeared that the table had the same purpose in the time of the dream, though the equipment was older.

The man in the dream brushed dust aside to expose the outline of a panel in the wooden wall. Kraw had wondered as a child why there had been a wooden wall in the cellar, for that same wall was still there, but his father had said it had simply been left over from a change in the hall above and too good to cast aside. Kraw had later learned that this was a lie, a lie to defend a secret.

His heart thumped, for he guessed what the man in

the dream would do.

Which meant that Kraw knew who he was.

Narkam, the viceroy who had served King Flammos, the tyrant of the dragon kings who had plunged Incendium into a reign of darkness.

Kraw watched Narkam's nimble fingers tap out a combination on the inlay blocks in the wall. Did he whisper a word? It seemed to Kraw that he did, but he preferred to think that it was the sequence of taps that opened the door. A word of such power would have been a spell, and Kraw didn't like to acknowledge the prospect of magic.

A small door opened to reveal a hiding spot, one lined with metal to protect its contents from any damage. It was filled with a strange pale mist. This was where the scroll disappeared. The door was sealed and then footfalls sounded on the stairs.

Narkam darted back into the hole in the floor, securing the grate from the underside and disappearing into the sewers well before anyone entered the cellar room. He made his way back through the passage, and Kraw knew he would emerge in another part of the city, then saunter home as if innocent.

It was at this moment that Kraw awakened, every detail clear in his mind. He stifled an urge each time to race to the family home and check the cellar. He had no time for such an errand, and it would be futile. He knew the contents of the scroll, of course. It was the mark of each apprentice to spontaneously write a copy of that scroll's contents. Kraw couldn't explain the mechanism to his own satisfaction. He didn't believe in magic, but given the confession in the scroll, that might have been what caused the automatic writing. He tried to avoid thinking about it, for the scroll's message and the legacy defied everything Kraw believed to be true.

Yet it was true, as well.

Why did the dream come to him now? King Ouros didn't invite an era of darkness with his reign—in fact, he couldn't be more different than his forebear Flammos. Was it a warning that the ancient treason of the viceroy would have consequences? Was it simply guilt for the act of his forebear? Kraw tossed and turned, convinced that he was going to die. The dream seemed to warn him that the responsibility for the viceroy would pass and soon.

He itched to check upon the scroll, but felt the dream was sufficient warning to leave it be. What if the dream had been inflicted upon him to compel him to reveal the scroll? Kraw would not do it.

Besides, he couldn't check on the scroll without arousing curiosity. He himself lived in the palace in his own apartments and had done so since becoming viceroy. Kraw's younger brother and wife lived in the house with their children and grandchildren, as well as with a few cousins and more distant relations. Since he had come to the post young, he had not been married and had no children of his own. Once he had accepted the post, he had had no time for such matters. The administration of the palace had been his life.

One of his brother's sons should be Kraw's heir, but he delayed the choice. Ranaj, the older boy, now a man, had a certain charm but showed little attention to detail. That trait would not serve him well in a household of dragon shifters. Saraw, the second, had high expectations of himself and was unlikely to work hard, another trait that would lead to failure. Kraw didn't think either of them had any commitment to anyone beyond themselves and their own comfort. He wouldn't have put them in charge of a chicken coop, let alone a royal palace.

He had always liked Jarak's third son, despite that boy's rebellious youth. Arkan had appeared to have a gift for finding trouble or making it, but love had set him on the right path. Kraw thought it a sign that his nature was essentially good. Arkan's wife had died in childbirth, though, leaving him with two young children. Arkan had sufficient responsibilities for a few years, managing his duties to the family business along with those energetic children.

Could Kraw's choice not wait?

The dream's persistence, though, made him fear the time had come.

King Ouros should have been content.

Instead, he was uneasy.

As was his habit in such times, he reviewed his blessings. They were plentiful.

His oldest daughter, Drakina, had not only married her Carrier of the Seed in an official ceremony but had born a son, Gravitas, who was both healthy and a dragon shifter. Against every expectation, his defiant daughter had fulfilled the traditional responsibility of the eldest child, and Ouros had an official heir.

Drakina would not have been the daughter he knew and loved if she had not conceived the child before the wedding, but Ouros was past the moment of quibbling. Indeed, if the execution of her first betrothed and some early affection with her HeartKeeper was the sum of her rebellion, Ouros knew how lucky he was. For centuries, he had expected Drakina to challenge the law of succession and insist that a daughter should be as entitled to inherit as a son. He felt as if he had avoided a conflagration.

His second daughter, Gemma, had secured an alliance with Regalia, the sister planet of Incendium, by marrying its king. Ouros supposed that he should have anticipated that strategic marriage to proceed a little differently from his plans: Gemma had married Urbanus, the heir, but his twin brother, Venero, had proven to be her Carrier of the Seed.

There was no denying the call of the Seed, Ouros knew that, so he had few regrets about the resolution. It could have been much worse. Over the course of the pair's adventures upon Regalia, both Queen Arcana and Urbanus had died, so Venero had become king—both of Regalia and of Gemma's heart. Ouros did not doubt that his daughter, trained by the Warrior Maidens of Cumae, would make an excellent wife for Venero, given the unrest between factions in his newfound kingdom. The situation, too, contented him as a suitable fate for his second daughter.

The third daughter of the Incendium royal family was also married to her Carrier of the Seed and expecting a child. Ouros had not anticipated that Thalina would fall in love with an android, much less that she would aid Acion's evolution to a biological organism, and that made him feel foolish. Thalina had always loved machines better than people. Their union was, he had to admit, a perfect match.

Even if it had compelled him to overturn Scintillon's Law.

Ouros frowned. He didn't like changing laws, especially old ones, even when he suspected it was the right thing to do. He had a healthy respect for tradition and always felt that change was occurring too quickly when it happened at all. And he had never expected Thalina to be the one to compel him to reconsider anything.

She had her mother's stubborn nature, though.

Thalia was happy, which contented Ouros, too.

The android in question, Acion, had arrived on Incendium, charged to deliver a gift to Ouros himself. Since the freighter, the Archangel, had returned to port with Thalina and Acion, the gift had been inspected, examined, and finally delivered into the king's hands.

This gift and the disappearance of his seventh

daughter, Anguissa, captain of the Archangel, were the source of the king's concern. Ouros turned the clear cylinder in his hands, wondering yet again if he should release the creature trapped inside.

He had learned about ShadowCasters when he had been a young dragon, and they had been presumed extinct even then. It was a marvel to hold one, and he wondered whether the dark shape in the cylinder really was a ShadowCaster, or whether this was a hoax.

There was one way to find out.

ShadowCasters were an ancient life form and one said to be attuned to the vibrations of the future. Ouros forgot the speculation as to how they glimpsed into time ahead of the present: he'd always preferred facts over guesses, even educated guesses. He recalled a story that an emperor had ordered their destruction, after his enemies repeatedly anticipated his surprise attacks.

He held the cylinder to the light. The creature inside looked like a dead insect. It was black and motionless, unless he turned the cylinder and gravity dislodged it. Even then, it fell, as if inert. It didn't appear to be breathing or to have a pulse. Ouros shook the receptacle and it didn't respond.

Another king might have doubted its powers.

Ouros was a dragon king, and he wanted facts. He held up the cylinder and stared through it at his chambers, enjoying how the glass distorted the view. Was this how a ShadowCaster saw the future? Was it a question of perspective?

Would it tell him what had happened—or what was going to happen—to Anguissa? He had demanded the story of her disappearance twice from Thalina and hadn't liked it any better the second time. How like Anguissa to sacrifice herself for the sake of her sister and that sister's Carrier. Had she guessed that Acion was Thalina's HeartKeeper? Ouros was sure she had. Like the

ShadowCaster, Anguissa had an ability to anticipate future events with uncanny accuracy. She said it was only logical to see the results of one's actions. Ouros knew otherwise. That daughter, the bold one who challenged every expectation, had the confidence of knowing she would survive every feat.

Would she survive this one?

Would she have made the same choice, even if she'd known otherwise?

Ouros winced, knowing that his Anguissa wouldn't have changed a thing. His mother had always said that the prickly and outspoken people were the ones who cared the most. That was certainly true of Anguissa.

It could also be said to be true of his wife, although she was inclined to hide her sting.

Ouros felt Ignita's presence before he saw or smelled her.

"Are you going to release it?" she asked, and he glanced down to find her peering at the cylinder.

"Do you think I should?" He asked her a question, rather than answering, wanting to know her view.

"Whyever not?" She took the cylinder from his hand, peering at the creature within. "It was a gift. It must have come to you for a reason."

Ouros looked at her, intrigued. "You think it chooses its own course?"

Ignita smiled. "That's what I was taught. That a ShadowCaster had a way of ensuring it passed into the right hand at the right time. It saw its own future and made it come true."

What a notion. "To what end? To warn someone?"

"To make the future what it should be."

"According to whom?"

She handed him the vessel. "You'll have to ask the ShadowCaster that."

"Any word from Anguissa?"

A shadow touched his queen's brow. "No, but I wouldn't have expected any. We'll hear from her when she marches into the palace again."

"I hope it is soon."

Ignita placed her hand on Ouros' shoulder then gave it a little squeeze. "Don't tell me you're afraid to release a little dead millipede?" she teased, though he knew she understood his hesitation.

"You think it has something to tell us."

"I don't think it would be here otherwise."

Ouros nodded. "And maybe its counsel will tell us what to do to bring Anguissa home."

"Maybe. There's something that we have to do to shape the future as it should be, or the ShadowCaster wouldn't be here." Ignita's eyes lit with fire. "And if the future doesn't include every one of my daughters being safe and happy, the ShadowCaster will regret its choice."

Ouros smiled at her ferocity, though it was a good reminder. "We will release it in our dragon form," he said, and Ignita nodded agreement.

"In the royal audience chambers?"

"Yes, there's more room there, and after all, we *are* giving it an audience."

"Should we summon Kraw, so there is a witness?"

"That's an excellent idea."

"Don't you think he looks tired these days?" Ignita asked. "Should we insist that he take a vacation?"

"You know Kraw. He never takes a vacation, for he says I never do."

"Perhaps both of you should take a vacation."

"Let's see what the ShadowCaster says," Ouros demurred. "I'll send word to Kraw now and we can begin on the hour. Also, I'll have Kraw seal the chamber, so that the ShadowCaster cannot escape."

Soon he would have his fact.

Kraw, unlike the king and queen, felt a dislike for the ShadowCaster that he believed to be healthy. He didn't trust anything or anyone who poked into future events or claimed to know things they had no rational means of knowing. Dreams and portents were like the tricks played at the carnivals on unsuspecting fools, who deserved to be separated from their funds.

It smacked of that unwholesome practice, magic.

Kraw didn't even share the royal enthusiasm for astrologers, even though their craft was more science than art. In Kraw's view, the future could take care of itself. He ensured the present was all it could be, partly by keeping the past where it belonged. Still, a summons was a summons, so he had the audience chamber sealed and joined his king and queen there as promptly as possible.

His recurring dream had left him tired, irritable, and impatient with nonsense. That it was a similar kind of nonsense in his view only made him more cranky.

Of course, he hid his thoughts and feelings from his king and queen, who clearly had expectations of the ShadowCaster.

Kraw expected little of the black smudge in the bottom of the clear cylinder, but it was always a treat to see both the king and the queen shift shape. They were magnificent in their dragon forms, and the awe he felt when he witnessed the change always reminded him of his own splendid good fortune to serve them as he did.

The king was the first to shift, waiting only until the doors were locked behind Kraw before doing so. He had already given the vial containing the ShadowCaster to Queen Ignita, so threw out his arms and cast back his head. He was surrounded with a swirl of sparks even as his figure itself seemed to glow. In the blink of an eye, he reared above them in his dragon form and breathed a playful stream of fire at the ceiling. His scales were deep blue and gleamed when he moved, his power and agility undiminished even at his age. His belly scales could have been made of gold, given the way they shone. His nails were black, the feathers streaming from his wings were indigo, and his wings themselves were so dark a blue as to be close to black. There were swirls of gold on the tops of Ouros' wings, as if they had been painted there by a skillful artist. His eyes glittered like cut gems and he turned a look upon his wife that was both amorous and regal.

It had always seemed to Kraw that the character of the members of the royal family was more clear when they took their dragon forms. He felt more aware of their motivations when they were dragons. Ouros, for example, was motivated by love for his wife, his daughters, and his kingdom. When the king was in his dragon form, Kraw couldn't forget that truth. He knew they could be inscrutable, to him and to others, so maybe it was a case of them revealing themselves to him because they trusted him.

Ignita handed the vial to her husband, then spun in place. Sparks flew from her, seeming to light on the hem of her skirts as she turned, and her figure disappeared in a cloud of smoke. The cloud grew taller and wider, seeming to simmer from its very core, then her dragon form was revealed. Ignita looked softer than Ouros, if such a thing could be said of a dragon. Her scales were myriad shades of soft blue and purple and their edges were less clearly defined. She had more feathers, and they were opalescent and flowing, disguising her strength like veils on a dancer. There was fire in her eyes, though, a fire that a smart person wouldn't forget, and Kraw saw her devotion to her husband and daughters in her fierce expression.

He was a bachelor and contentedly so, but when Kraw saw the king and queen in their dragon forms, he wondered what it would be like to be adored by a dragon shifter. Did the object of affection feel like the prize gem of the dragon's hoard? Kraw wasn't a fanciful man, but he imagined so.

The pair faced each other, Ouros' tail swirling around Kraw protectively, then the king loosened the lid. "Are we prepared?" he asked, his voice more resonant and deep than when he was in human form.

Ignita nodded.

"Certainly, your majesty," Kraw said and bowed his head. He fingered his mustache, ensuring it was perfect, for he felt a sense of ceremony.

When he straightened, Ouros opened the vial to release the ShadowCaster.

Nothing happened.

Ouros made a little growl of frustration, then tipped the cylinder. The ShadowCaster slid out and dropped toward the floor, apparently lifeless.

"It'll be hurt!" Ignita cried and snatched for it.

The ShadowCaster slipped through her talons, though, for it exploded into a million tiny dark specks and fell like black rain toward the inlaid floor. All three observers caught their breath and took a step back. Kraw was aware the queen put a claw in one of the king's and that he drew her slightly behind himself.

But the black drops had his full attention. They turned course just above the floor, and swirled upward like a flock of birds. To Kraw's surprise, they formed an image of a sun, several planets and their moons, all rotating in place as if watched from several light years' distance.

"Fiero Four," Ouros breathed, naming the system in which Incendium was located.

"There's Incendium and Regalia," Ignita said with excitement. "And Sylvawyld!"

The dots swirled again, and Kraw had the impression that their vision zoomed in on Incendium. Next he saw the capital city and his heart sank at the realization that it was the same era as his recurring dream.

When the ShadowCaster showed Flammos on the throne, Kraw knew that his family secret was about to be revealed.

Perhaps he would have no reason to choose an apprentice, not once the treason of the viceroy's family was known by the king.

He sat down heavily, feeling every moment of his many years, and wondered if he would leave the audience chamber alive.

The dragon kings of Incendium had never taken treason lightly, no matter how justified the culprit might believe his actions to be.

Chapter Two

Arkan knew that his beloved Jalana would have appreciated the irony of his current situation. She had always insisted that her love had tamed the bad boy of Incendium city, and Arkan had never argued that truth with her. She had claimed his heart and he had changed his ways to capture hers in turn.

They had been so wonderfully happy that he had never regretted a thing.

But now she was gone, and he was left with Narjal and Tarun, who each echoed their mother in different ways, neither less potent than the other. Yet both also had his own rebellious nature, as if to ensure their father understood how much trouble he had been. Narjal, his daughter, was older and bolder. In fact, she was fearless and was forever leading her younger brother into trouble. Tarun had a mischievous streak of his own and the only thing that ensured Arkan's sanity was that they were too young to find real danger.

Yet.

He couldn't imagine how he would survive their teenage years. They were both attractive children—thanks to Jalana, in Arkan's view—and had a charm that helped them talk themselves out of the consequences of any act. Arkan knew that trait came from himself.

At the same time, he had become so responsible that

he barely recognized himself. Arkan had devoted himself to his family's business to ensure the financial security of his children. There hadn't been much of a place for him, since his older brothers had taken the better jobs. Ranaj was the public presence of their trading empire, so he attended all the best parties and knew all the best people and lived in a style to rival the King of Incendium himself. Saraw was the quieter one, who negotiated the deals—many of which Arkan had learned were not entirely legal. His brother was one for shortcuts, if he could turn a better profit with them or return to his own amusements more quickly, and Arkan seemed to be the only one troubled by these choices.

Knowing he was reliant upon their goodwill, he was compelled to remain silent.

He had done odd jobs for his father, but shortly after Jalana's death, his mother had taken pity upon him and decided to retire. Or maybe she had chosen to test him. Arkan had never been sure. Either way, the task of bookkeeping had become available to him then, and though the adding of columns in the back room was as far from his dreams as any job could be, he'd taken it.

For his kids.

He'd been prepared to hate his job, but he actually enjoyed it. There was something refreshing about that addition of columns and tallying of items. The numbers never lied, and they often gave insight into other issues. He liked how rational it all was, how finite, and how lacking in mystery or suspense it was. Everything happened for a reason and there were no arbitrary choices. Ventures lost money because of overspending, bad budgeting, or poor management, not random incidents that changed everything.

Like a healthy woman's sudden death in childbirth.

It was good to live in the family home, too, for he had fond memories of his own childhood there. The estate was large, and the house was rambling, courtesy of centuries of additions and modifications. It seemed that every corner promised a forgotten cranny or a hidden passageway, plus there were books and games, cousins and pets. Arkan liked that there were many servants and many eyes on his mischievous children. They were safe. They were healthy. They had opportunities to learn and there would be more as they grew older. That was Arkan's true compensation.

He hoped Jalana was proud of him and the life he'd made for them.

His mother laughed at him when Narjal and Tarun found trouble, insisting that the past revisited the future. She thought he deserved the challenges they gave him, and maybe he did. If nothing else, his life gave Arkan a new perspective.

Arkan's family had filled the post of viceroy at the palace since the days of King Scintillon, the responsibility passing through the male line of the family. When there wasn't a son, a brother or nephew would take the post, each new viceroy carefully trained by the last. It was considered a responsibility of the others to marry and have children, in order to ensure that the post was never in risk of being left vacant.

Uncle Kraw had taken the post while comparatively young, since his father had married late. Arkan's father, Jarak, was the younger son from that late match, and he had married then fathered three sons. Kraw had been viceroy for longer than Arkan had been alive, and Arkan had been raised with the assumption that one of his older brothers would be groomed by Kraw to take his place.

The family had built its own trade over the centuries, and Arkan didn't doubt that some early success had been due to the favor of the crown. Now, though, they managed a financial empire, trading in currencies, financing expeditions and equipment, and investing in future endeavors. Arkan spent most of his days in the counting room in the family home, which was a far more cheerful place than might have been anticipated. It was a sunny room, the windowsills lush with plants from Incendium and other locations.

It was also oppressively quiet when his kids were elsewhere. Arkan preferred when they played in the counting room while he worked, but they had recently begun to have lessons. Narjal was ten years old and Tarun was six. Arkan had taught them himself to this point, but it was time, his mother had announced, for them to be tamed—as much as might be possible.

The children hadn't embraced the change any better than their father had. Arkan suspected that the tutor had already come to the conclusion that they could not be tamed. Narjal orchestrated daily escapes from their lessons, ensuring the pair disappeared while the tutor's back was turned, and substituting daring adventures of her own for their lessons. She had taken Tarun to the zoo unaccompanied, been caught investigating the sewers with her younger brother, and had even—probably at Tarun's insistence—gotten them both to the star station and aboard a shuttle to the starport before being retrieved.

In a way, Arkan admired how enterprising she was.

In another, her inventiveness made him dread the future even more.

So, he wasn't truly surprised when the tutor rapped at the door of the counting room one morning, flushed and flustered. "I won't do it anymore," she announced before Arkan could greet her. "I won't be responsible for those *heathens*."

Arkan stood. "You mean my children?" He decided against noting that their religious beliefs were of no relevance.

"Of course, I mean your children!" she sputtered.

"They are outrageously disobedient..."

"But that is why they have lessons."

The tutor pointed a finger at him, her outrage clear. "I have endured sufficient insolence from those little monsters to last me the rest of my days. I don't believe they *can* be taught, especially as they continue to disappear..."

"Disappear?" Arkan stepped forward, anticipating the worst. "Where have they been gone?"

"How should I know? They are sneaky and cunning beyond their years, especially that girl. Oh, she looks pretty enough, but she is devious and wicked..."

"And I think it is time for our ways to part," Arkan said firmly. "If you're so convinced that my children are evil, I doubt that you will be able to teach them effectively."

"I am not the problem in this situation!"

"How long have they been gone?" Arkan asked, wanting to calculate how far they might have gone.

"Perhaps half an hour," the tutor admitted, her tone still irritated. "Fortunately, I ensured that the doors and gates were sealed before our lessons began this morning."

"So they must still be in the house?" There were still plenty of opportunities for trouble to be found.

"They are hiding," she said grimly. "I've been looking for them, without success."

Arkan tapped his desktop to secure his files, then left the counting room with purpose. The door was locked behind him with a touch. "Where have you looked?" he asked without glancing back.

"The kitchen, the yard, their bedrooms, the playroom, the garage, the storeroom..."

Arkan thought of the sewers. "The cellar?"

Her expression was all the answer he needed. "I won't do it anymore!" she shouted after him, but Arkan didn't stop.

"Speak to my mother, then. She hired you."

The tutor snorted but Arkan was racing down the stairs to the main floor of the house. The mess after the sewer adventure meant that he didn't want a repetition. He stormed through the kitchen and down the stairs in the storeroom, activating a light on his way.

The cellar appeared to be empty.

But there was the clean scent of his children's soap and the vessels on the worktable looked to be jumbled. He could even see a small handprint, disturbing the dust on one, but he didn't let his gaze linger on it.

They were here and they were hiding.

Watching.

It was time to change the rules of the game. Arkan bent down to examine the sewer grate as if it had been the reason for his arrival. He rattled it, but it was secured. He sighed with evident relief.

"Thank Yarkella," he said, as if he had only come to check the sewer. He straightened and returned to the stairs. "They're not here," he called, though he doubted the tutor had followed him. "Let's check the garage. Tarun is fascinated by that new velocitor." He climbed the stairs, extinguishing the light on his way, but didn't step into the kitchen. Instead, he opened the door and closed it again, remaining in the shadows at the summit of the stairs. Because there was a bend in the stairs, they wouldn't be able to see what he had done.

His eyes adjusted quickly to the darkness and he was able to discern the gleam of the bottles in which the wine fermented. The silence didn't last very long.

"We fooled him!" Narjal whispered in triumph. "Now we have to finish before he comes back."

"We can't move the table," Tarun whispered. "It's too heavy."

"We have to find a way. There's a secret treasure there!"

"We should have asked Pater to help."

"We can't. It's a *secret.*" Narjal's tone made her opinion of her brother's objections clear.

"How can you even know it's there if it's a secret?"

"I *know,*" Narjal insisted with such conviction that Arkan shivered. How could she know?

"You could be wrong. You were before."

"We'll never be sure unless we look!"

"I want to see the velocitor."

"Be quiet and help, then I'll take you to the velocitor."

A light illuminated far below Arkan. He guessed that Narjal had taken a handheld light source for her adventure and peeked to see that he was right. The children had their backs to him and the light shone upon the old wooden wall. Narjal had already moved most of the vessels aside and was kneeling on the old worktable. Tarun crouched behind her and she handed him the light.

"Shine it there. That's where the secret hiding place is."

"How do you know?"

"I do!"

Tarun did as instructed, and Narjal ran her hands over the wooden partition. Arkan sat on the steps to watch her, intrigued. He had been fascinated by that wall when he was a kid, too, though his father had told him to leave it alone.

Was there a reason why?

"Look!" Narjal sat back, triumphant, having found the perimeter of a door in the wall. She blew the dust out of the crack and ran her fingertip around the edge. "Just like in the book," she whispered in awe.

"What book?"

"The one I found. The *magic* book."

Arkan frowned. There was no such thing as magic. There was deception and there was nonsense. They weren't on Regalia with its superstitions and primitive thinking! He might have interjected, but decided to let Narjal's venture fail first.

"So, open it," Tarun said.

Narjal lifted her hands. She murmured something under her breath three times, then waited. Nothing happened, just as Arkan had expected. She dug at the perimeter of the door with her fingers, but it didn't budge.

Maybe it wasn't even a door.

"I knew we should have gone to the velocitor," Tarun said with disgust and turned to jump from the table.

Then Narjal gasped. Arkan gasped himself for the insignia of the dragon kings of Incendium appeared on the wooden panel. It looked to be drawn with fire and the flames crackled, glowing brilliant orange in the darkness. The flames faded and the insignia appeared to be branded on the door. A waft of smoke rose from the wood as Arkan heard a sizzle. Then the door opened and white mist spilled forth from the space behind it. Arkan thought he could see a pile of scrolls within it.

Narjal reached a hand into the mist, both fearless and foolish.

Arkan leaped down the stairs and snatched her up. She cried out in protest, and Tarun ran for the stairs. "I'm going to see the velocitor," he said and scampered out of sight. No doubt, he thought Narjal was in trouble and wanted to avoid being implicated.

"We have to look inside," she insisted.

"We do not," Arkan said firmly. "What book did you find? Where is it?"

"It's in the library. It was hidden at the back of the shelves and I read it. It's a spell book."

"You know there's no such thing as magic."

His daughter was defiant. "I know there *is*. The spell worked."

Arkan tried a different tack. "You know that the practice of magic is illegal on Incendium."

"Because it works. Because *that* worked." She gestured to the open door, which continued to spill white mist. The mist pooled on the floor of the cellar, as if it were heavy, and flowed toward the sewer grate in the floor. At the flick of her hand, the door slammed shut and Arkan watched its perimeter fade from view.

Surely his daughter hadn't made the door close from a distance with a gesture?

Surely his daughter couldn't have any *powers*?

No, it was a coincidence. It had to be. The door had just closed at the same time.

Narjal squirmed out of his grip and climbed back onto the worktable, trying to find the door again. He quickly saw that she couldn't—and the murmuring of her spell yielded no results. He was relieved then, that his fears had been mistaken.

She turned on him, outraged. "You did this, Pater! It's hidden again because you don't believe."

"Maybe it never really existed," he said, noting how the mist had disappeared from view. "Maybe you imagined it."

Narjal's expression turned stubborn. "Maybe I need to read more."

"No," Arkan said. "You're going to give me that book and you're going to abandon this adventure."

"But..."

"Or I'll make you take twice as many lessons as before, in a locked room."

Her lips set. "I could get out of it."

Arkan bent down to look her in the eye. "If you put as much effort into your lessons as you do in evading them, you'd be done early enough to play whatever games you wanted."

She smiled then, a sweet smile too much like Jalana's,

and wrinkled her nose. "It's boring."

"Of course, it's boring. It's good training for becoming an adult."

"I don't want to be an adult."

"I don't like it much, either." Arkan lifted her up and held her on his hip. "You're getting bigger, though. I won't be able to lift you soon."

She kissed his cheek. "Of course you will, Pater. You're the strongest man of all."

"Hmm, flattery," he teased. "You just don't want to give me that book."

"I thought you might forget."

"Not a chance. We'll get it now, then you'll forget all of this nonsense."

"Does magic have to be nonsense?"

"Yes, it does, because it is." Arkan spoke with more confidence than he was feeling in this moment. What had happened with that door? He disliked that he couldn't think of a rational explanation.

Narjal sighed and Arkan knew the argument wasn't over. If he had the book, though, and her spell didn't work on the door in the cellar, then maybe she'd soon get bored with this particular adventure.

He could only hope.

In the meantime, he would go and talk to Uncle Kraw when he had a spare day, just in case there was something important about that hidden hiding place. That it had shown the insignia of the king for a moment indicated that Kraw was the most likely to know the truth.

He doubted it was important, given that it was hidden in the cellar.

Ignita watched the ShadowCaster with fascination. The creature divided itself into thousands if not millions of small dark dots, then moved to arrange images. It was like watching the vid, but with no color.

Deborah Cooke

It took them into the streets of Incendium city, which were seething with discontent. They had the perspective of someone walking through the city and Ignita shivered as the sense of unease and violence that permeated the vision. People muttered about new laws and injunctions, though none dared to express a complaint against King Flammos.

They had learned the consequences of that quickly enough.

She recalled her history lessons, the ones given to her as soon as she and Ouros had become betrothed. Her family believed that no bride should be unprepared for the world she would make her own, so she had crammed facts about Incendium's history until she suspected she knew more of it than her intended. She remembered the cruelty of Flammos well, driven by his conviction that all conspired against him.

The vision ducked into a tavern on the far side of Incendium, in the rough area beyond the star port. They entered the tavern, and Ignita's eyes widened at the disreputable people there, the foreigners from other worlds, and the conspicuous consumption of stimulants both legal and illegal. She thought she could smell the filth of the place, and she saw credits in a dozen currencies being exchanged. The vision trailed into a back room, slipping through a barred door, where two men sat at a table.

"Embron and Blazion," she said without meaning to speak aloud.

Ouros glanced at her. "The younger sons of Rubeo? The twins?"

"There is an image in the archives."

He nodded, turning his attention back to the ShadowCaster's display. The pair conferred, their heads bent together and their voices low. Ignita heard the words "rebellion," "coup," and "justice."

It seemed that Flammos' conviction that his younger brothers had been conspiring against him was true. A servant entered the room, bringing a fresh pitcher of whatever brew the brothers consumed and a steaming platter of food. Another man entered and the brothers straightened, stepped forward to shake his hand.

"A conspirator," Ouros murmured.

The servant left and the ShadowCaster's vision followed him. He cast aside his apron and left the tavern, hastening to the palace. At the kitchen door, he murmured a word and was admitted, shown down a dark passageway, then thrust into a chamber where King Flammos awaited him. He was playing with a stack of credits. The man fell to his knees and began to speak in haste.

"A traitor to the twin princes," Ignita said softly.

The vision swirled and they were at the starport, where a small vessel was being outfitted. It was isolated, at the end of a long row of empty gates. A woman with hair as white as snow strode down the corridor to the gate. She was young, despite the hue of her hair, dressed like a star captain and moved with confidence. She was not armed. There was a shimmer surrounding her, and Ignita watched with curiosity as she approached the guarded gate of the isolated vessel.

She blew a kiss to each of the guards, but they remained impassive. She walked directly past them, along the gangplank, and onto the vessel, but they took no notice of her. They certainly didn't stop her.

"An intruder," Ouros said.

"A witch," Ignita corrected, being more inclined to see sorcery than her husband.

"There's no such thing," he chided.

"Then how did she do that?"

He glanced at her, frowned, then turned back to the display. "There is always a rational explanation, even if it's not immediately evident."

Ignita held her tongue. They saw the twin princes then, being brought to the vessel in chains and shackles. They were forced aboard and the portal was secured, before the armed troops retreated.

The ShadowCaster swirled again and showed King Flammos in his chamber, watching a massive but primitive display of the sky. It took up the better part of a wall, but the resolution was less than was typical now. Ignita noted that motion upon the screen was in increments instead of flowing smoothly. A solitary vessel left its gate and moved to the jump zone.

"Presumably it was controlled remotely," Ouros said.

A distant voice counted down, then the vessel surged into the jump zone. There was a flash and it disappeared. King Flammos saluted the screen with his cup then drained it, his satisfaction more than clear.

The dots moved, as if the focus shifted from the king to the shadows behind him. In the darkness, a man's figure became clear, his features unfamiliar but the mark of the viceroy upon his uniform.

"Of course, his viceroy attends him," Ouros said and frowned. "Who is that, Kraw?"

"Narkam, sir."

Ouros shrugged. "I don't remember anything about him. I shall have to do some research."

The ShadowCaster became a whirlwind of tiny dots, and they spiraled down into the cylindrical vessel. They congealed into a single small black organism, one that looked like a dead millipede, and stilled.

"That's it?" Ouros cried when the creature didn't move again. "But we know all that! What possible relevance does this have to the present and the future?" He growled and smoke emanated from his nostrils as he snatched up the cylinder and shook it. "What about Anguissa?" he roared, but the ShadowCaster remained still. Ouros turned to Ignita. "It must be about Narkam! That was the only detail I didn't know."

But Ignita was more concerned that the viceroy suddenly slumped to the floor, his face pale. "Kraw! Ouros, something is wrong with Kraw!"

Chapter Three

After a visit to the velocitor and an argument with his mother, Arkan returned to the counting room to finish his work for the day. He had the so-called spell book that Narjal had found in the library, but a quick fan through it had revealed that the pages were all blank. Undoubtedly, a rational explanation for her experience would reveal itself.

If Tarun had been older, he might have thought it a prank played by one sibling on the other. Maybe one of his nieces or nephews were responsible.

The truth would come out, Arkan was sure of it.

He settled at his desk and made to open his desktop display. Instead, he found himself reaching for a quill. He hadn't written by hand in years, but had a curious urge to do as much. He found some paper in the desk and pulled out a clean white sheet.

How strange. Why did he feel such a compulsion? It was another thing he couldn't explain. He lifted the quill, rolling it in his hand as he recalled the feel of it. He touched it to the paper and words began to flow into the page, as quickly as he could write them.

Arkan had no idea where they were coming from. He read them for the first time as he wrote them down, and as he wrote what proved to be a long message, his eyes widened in surprise.

I, Narkam, *viceroy of Incendium, sworn to the service of King Flammos, have committed treason and betrayed the trust of the king. Though I believe my actions to have been justified, I also recognize that they were illegal and subject to the most severe justice of the king. I also violated the sanctions against the use of magic on Incendium, for I saw no other means to save the kingdom. I was driven to this by my discovery that the king has done evil to protect his throne and though I know I have overstepped my bounds, I could do nothing else.*

In the Incendium year 208, King Rubeo gained his majority of eight-one years of age became King of Incendium. Rubeo had five children by his HeartKeeper, Bellica. Flammos was eldest and heir, born in 307. A daughter, Aurora, was born in 310 and a second daughter, Lustra, was born in 314. In 317, the queen delivered twin boys, Blazion and Embron.

My service to the crown commenced in 554, and Aurora and Lustra were already dead. I knew they had died before coming of age. I did not know, until Prince Flammos confided in me one night after a drunken binge in Incendium city, that he had killed them with his own talons. He was proud of his deed and gloated of his cleverness as I helped him to his apartment. The hatred that spewed from him when he was unchecked was shocking. In the morning, he had no recollection of his confession, but I quietly confirmed several details over the following days, and was convinced of his guilt.

The crime however was years in the past, and I had only his own confession as evidence. I continued to serve in silence, for I feared dismissal from my post—or worse—if I raised the question with King Rubeo. The prince appeared to embark upon a course of greater honor and less indulgence. I hoped he had learned from the past.

Upon Rubeo's death in 577, Flammos became king and any hope that his habits had changed was quickly proven wrong. Incendium was cast into a pit of ruin with each day bringing more injustice and infamy to this great kingdom. I had heard whispers that Blazion and Embron meant to challenge their older brother over the crown, but evidently Flammos heard them as well. He ordered that his two brothers be cast into space with no supplies, a death sentence that would leave his talons clean. Perhaps he does recall that confession and my silence, for he gives the appearance of trusting me. Perhaps his trust is an illusion, intended to trap me. I cannot say. But he left the arrangements to me and I seized the opportunity to undermine his plan.

I knew that the king would not be easily deceived and I suspected that I would be watched. I planned for the princes, Blazion and Embron, to survive their banishment into space, by contriving that they should secretly be put into stasis. I equipped the ship myself with a prototype of the Fractal Interstellar Drive, but I needed help to send them to their fate.

I confided in one person, solely because I had need of her services. She is, against all expectation, a Regalian and one skilled in sorcery. I heard she was living in the forests beyond Incendium city and I approached her under the guise of imperial investigation. Instead of charging and arresting her, which would lead to her certain death, I offered her the opportunity to survive Incendium's justice. If she cast the spell to shield my actions from the scrutiny of the king and all others, and went with the princes upon their journey, I would ensure that she was not discovered.

She laughed at me. I thought she might decline, but she said she had anticipated my arrival. I couldn't make sense of this for I had chosen to approach her on a whim, but she was confident. Alluring, as well. She countered my offer, expressing her willingness to fulfill it but insisting that her price would be twofold: first, I was forbidden to tell the princes anything about her, and secondly, her spell would place a curse upon my lineage. My son and his son and all through the ages forevermore would be compelled to remember my treason. In this way, we would be the keepers of the secret that could betray us all. I took her wager, for I didn't believe in curses, and it was arranged.

Before taking the post of viceroy, I worked in the engineering labs of Incendium. In order to guarantee that no one could track the vessel carrying the princes after its departure, I added a random number generator to the Fractal Interstellar Drive. There is no *telling where or when the princes will make landfall. The witch insisted that the drive was unnecessary, that her spell would bend time as well as impede discovery, but we each made our preparations. The princes are gone, but they remain reliant upon the spell of the witch who journeys with them, and unaware of it. There is much risk in their unwitting adventure, but I console myself that they have some small chance of survival.*

I have come to rely upon the witch myself and hope for her success.

I also am haunted by my deeds. As the king becomes more dissolute and more demanding, I fear for the future of Incendium. Perhaps my deceit is part of a sickness that will claim us all and reduce this once-mighty kingdom to ruin.

I believed the witch's curse was nonsense, but as I write this confession in the counting room of our family home, my son is writing it verbatim in another chamber of the house. When I halt, he halts. When I resume, he resumes. He has no knowledge of what I am writing, I didn't even tell him that I was writing, but he showed me his copy of my confession when I went to the kitchens for refreshment. It chilled me to read my own words in his hand, when he could have no knowledge of them. The witch was right. My will be my apprentice and I will hide the two scrolls in the cellar as she suggested. I suspect she was also correct that each viceroy after me will keep silent for the sake of his own survival and that we will be complicit for generation after generation.

The dragon kings of Incendium have long memories and no tolerance of treason. They will not suffer the discover of it in the family that serves in the most trusted role of their administration. If this truth is ever uncovered, I would hope that the king is held by a more temperate dragon than now, and that the preservation of the royal lineage will be rewarded.

In these dark days for Incendium, I am reassured by the hope that the princes live on in another land, with the honor and integrity that their father instilled within them.

I sign this confession of my own guilt in the ninth month of the year 589 in the city of Incendium.

Narkam
Viceroy of Incendium

Arkan read it twice, then ran a fingertip across the signature.

Could it be true? It seemed fantastic.

And yet, he had no idea where these words had originated.

He thought of the hiding place in the cellar and Narjal's book and frowned. He took the scroll and the book and headed for the palace. There was only one person who could tell him more, and that was his Uncle Kraw.

Arkan came.

Night was falling over the city of Incendium, and Kraw watched the light change outside the windows. It was his favorite time of day, when Incendium went to sleep, the sky changed hue, and the starport shone high above with new radiance. He had been brought to his apartment and settled in bed. He had been examined and fussed over and had managed to reveal nothing of the shock to him of the ShadowCaster's message.

King Ouros didn't understand the message now, but Kraw was certain his king would dig deeper and discover the truth. The king was persistent and would dig into the records until he was satisfied. The old secret would be revealed.

Would he die first? Kraw didn't know. He had no desire to die, but at the same time, he didn't want to face the fury of a dragon king who realized he'd been deceived. Ouros was inclined to rage first and be temperate later.

When his nephew's arrival was announced, Kraw felt a relief to his very toes. He was glad to no longer be alone in this responsibility. Arkan had always been clever.

Maybe the younger man would find an alternative solution. Kraw was tired and the prospect of having an apprentice cheered him.

"Are you well, Uncle?" Arkan asked with concern, no doubt surprised to find Kraw in his chambers and in bed.

"I am better now that you have arrived." Kraw sat up with an effort. "Secure the door and silence the comm, please."

Arkan's eyes narrowed. "Then you know."

"I have been waiting."

When his instructions had been followed, the younger man presented a scroll of paper to his uncle. "How did I do this?"

"It is the curse."

"But there are no curses and there is no magic..."

"That's what I thought, until it happened to me."

Arkan sat back with a frown. "I don't like it. I don't trust it."

"It doesn't seem to care. You've been chosen as my apprentice..."

"No! I thought one of my brothers..."

"And you thought incorrectly. Neither Ranaj nor Saraw have the skill or the inclination that best serves a viceroy. Ranaj is too outspoken to be in close service to a dragon king, while Saraw is not burdened by integrity. Leave them to manage the family trade, while you serve the kingdom. My life has been spent in service to Incendium, and gladly so. I know the demands of the post, and I think it is a position that will suit you best of my three nephews."

"Tell me why, Uncle." Arkan held Kraw's gaze. "The real reason why."

Kraw saw no reason to be coy. "Because you are due to have your toes held to the fire. No woman will do it, not since Jalana's death, so it will have to be dragons."

"But the children..."

"Will be raised as if they were royalty themselves. They would have every opportunity to improve themselves. I think it would be ideal for them."

Arkan's lips set. "They could find an infinite amount of trouble."

Kraw smiled. "Yet they would have thousands more eyes upon them." His nephew appeared to consider that. Kraw nodded. "I'm glad you were chosen, Arkan. I never wanted to have to train Ranaj or Saraw."

"But they're older. Surely..."

"You have been chosen." Kraw shook the piece of paper at him. "It's uncontestable." He shouldn't have said it that way, he realized as much as soon as the words left his mouth, because Arkan's expression turned stubborn.

"What if I don't want to do it? What if I decline?"

"No one declines. Why would you?"

Arkan grimaced and leaned closer, lowering his voice when he spoke. "Because of Narjal. She found what she calls a book of spells, but when she gave it to me, its pages were blank."

"So, it isn't a spell book. Children are fanciful."

"She opened a hidden door in the wooden wall in the cellar with one of the spells she'd learned. There were scrolls within it, and smoke emanated from it, and the seal of the dragon kings burned on the door before it disappeared. She even closed it with a flick of her hand, from across the room. I saw it all."

Kraw was taken aback. Surely there couldn't be a witch in his own family? Was this a new manifestation of the curse? It seemed as if the secret was determined to be revealed, given his dream and the ShadowCaster and now Narjal. He knew his tone sharpened. "Who else saw this?"

"Only Tarun and me." Arkan sat back. "She'll do it again. Why wouldn't she? And I'd rather she didn't break

Incendium's law in a place where there are thousands of eyes watching her." He shook his head. "I must decline, Uncle. In fact, I think I should move out of the capital city with the children, just in case."

"But where will you go?"

"I don't know." Arkan shoved a hand through his hair. "It was only when I entered the palace that I realized the peril of the situation. All this power. All these ears and eyes. I have to protect her, Uncle."

"Of course, you do." Kraw cleared his throat. "But have you considered that the safest place for her might be here, in the palace?"

"How could that be?"

"It is human nature and that of dragons, too, to offer mercy to those they love."

Arkan's gaze locked with Kraw's. "Then why do we keep this secret?" he asked, indicating the scroll.

It was a good question. "Because the mercy may be preceded by fire."

Arkan rose to his feet and paced the width of the room, then sat down to confront Kraw once more. He had made a choice, and while Kraw admired that it was made quickly, he hoped it was the decision he desired most. "There can be no more curse from the past. There can be no more secret."

"What do you mean?"

Arkan flicked the scroll with his fingertip. "I will not leave this legacy for my children. Either we show this to the king and his inclination for mercy is proven to me for once and for all, or I will leave the city forever."

Kraw's stomach churned at the suggestion. "What about becoming my apprentice?"

"I'm still thinking about it. I need to be sure before I give my word."

Kraw didn't know what to say. While he admired Arkan's need to protect his children, he didn't think the curse left a lot of choice to the intended apprentice. He could see that his nephew was determined to proceed his own way and wished he could convince him to make a promise first.

He might confess all to the king then still be left without an apprentice.

He could lose everything.

Why did the curse make such demands now?

Kraw might have argued but there was a knock upon the door to his apartment.

"Can't you ignore it?" Arkan said with an echo of his own frustration.

Kraw smiled. "I am at the disposal of the king, remember. Will you go?"

"Of course." Arkan strode to the door, his impatience clear, and Kraw wondered what King Ouros would make of his manner. It was far from respectful. Perhaps the king would refuse to have Arkan as viceroy.

But then his nephew opened the door and a woman's low voice carried to Kraw's ears.

"Uncle Kraw!" Narjal cried, racing to his room and casting herself across the bed. "You're sick!"

"I'm just having a nap," Kraw said, not in the least bit surprised that Tarun climbed onto the bed after his sister. "And having you two visit is the very best way to wake up."

Arkan didn't return, nor did his voice rise in anger. Kraw listened and realized it had been the Princess Enigma who had brought the children to his apartment. That Arkan lingered to speak with her was a very, very good sign.

Enigma might change Arkan's mind as Kraw could not.

He decided to give the boy as much time as he needed and invited the children to settle in on either side of him.

"We followed Pater," Narjal confided. "He took my book."

"Oh? Was it a good book?" Kraw asked, knowing exactly which book she meant.

"The very best book," she agreed. "I want it back."

"Perhaps it should be a secret," Kraw suggested quietly and her dark gaze flew to his.

"He told you about it."

"He did, and I remember a story about it."

"There's a story?" Tarun asked, his eyes alight.

"There's always a story," Kraw said. "Let me tell you this one."

"I hope it has velocitor," Tarun said.

"I hope it ends happily," Narjal said.

"It does," Kraw acknowledged to Narjal, even as he tried to think of a way to satisfy Tarun, too. "You see, once there was a witch from Regalia and she was all alone on Incendium." He raised a finger. "Except, of course, for her velocitor, which was very fast..."

Arkan had always wondered whether a hint of dragon had crept into his family bloodline over the centuries. There wasn't enough of it that any of the viceroy's relations could shift shape or breathe fire, but Arkan had always known his family was different.

He had that certainty again when Uncle Kraw spotted the scroll. For a brief moment, there was a gleam of surprise in the viceroy's eyes, followed quickly by satisfaction, and then the older man's expression had become inscrutable. That look put Arkan in mind of a dragon guarding his hoard. Kraw held his gaze steadily, without revealing one increment of his thoughts, for what seemed like eternity.

As usual, Arkan blinked first.

He had been shocked to find his uncle in bed in the early evening, but supposed he was getting older. As a boy, he'd been awed by Uncle Kraw's elaborate mustache, his pride and joy, and it was still perfectly groomed. The older man seldom visited the family home, but when he did, his summary of his activities at the palace left everyone wide-eyed in wonder at his efficiency and the scope of his responsibilities.

Arkan had always been pretty sure his uncle confessed only a tiny increment of what he did, which only made his need to rest more reasonable.

"Because you are due to have your toes held to the fire. No woman will do it, not since Jalana's death, so it will have to be dragons."

There had been a glint of humor in the older man's eyes, a dare and a challenge both, and something that again reminded Arkan of dragons. He was tempted, very tempted, but he was afraid for Narjal, too.

His thoughts were spinning when the rap came at the door. He was both glad to have something to do, even as simple as answering a door, and irritated to have their conversation interrupted. He felt a need to choose immediately, and a sense that it would be prudent to delay.

"Yes?" Arkan said as he opened the door.

"Pater!" Narjal cried, hugged him, then pushed past him in search of Kraw. Tarun shot after his sister, moving quickly enough that Arkan barely managed to brush his fingertips across the top of the boy's head.

"I do apologize," the woman accompanying them said, and Arkan looked at her for the first time. Her hair was long and dark, falling in waves over her shoulders. Her eyes were dark and thickly lashed, her lips curved as if she enjoyed a private joke. There was a glint of amusement in her eyes yet a bit of concern as well. Her voice was low and luscious, her beauty enough to make his heart stop cold.

Sultry was the word that came to his mind.

Mysterious.

Belatedly, he realized who he was speaking to. "Your highness," Arkan said and bowed. "Princess Enigma, the vid doesn't do you credit."

She laughed a little. "Oh, you flatter as Kraw does. Are you related?"

"I am Arkan, Kraw's nephew."

"I am pleased to meet you. Will you be his apprentice then? My father has been wondering when Kraw would choose."

"We are discussing it." Arkan glanced back without meaning to do so, and looked at the princess again to find understanding in her dark gaze.

"You are concerned about the children," she guessed. "But many children have grown up happily in Incendium palace."

"I wouldn't mean to suggest otherwise..."

"She told me about her book," the princess said, interrupting him smoothly. "I know Incendium's laws as well as you do."

Their gazes met and held. Arkan swallowed, knowing it had been a long time since he had been so aware of a woman.

A dragon princess.

He should take the children and leave the city, for the sake of all of them.

Enigma smiled, just a little. "I was interested in her story, actually," she said. "I have a fascination with the intersection of the rational and the irrational, the meeting point, if you will, between magic and science."

"Is there one?"

"Of course there is! So often, what is labeled magic is simply science we have yet to understand. Is it magic to change shape from a woman to a dragon by force of will?"

"No, it's a perfectly reasonable transformation, more

than adequately explained."

"Here on Incendium. On other planets, in other systems, I might be perceived to be a magical being." She smiled and Arkan couldn't argue with a single thing she said.

"I suppose there are other examples," he ventured.

"Like recognizing someone's role in your life at first glimpse?" she said, then reached out her hand. A spark leaped from her fingertip to him, sizzling when it touched him. Arkan jumped, then a warm heat spread through his body, as if he had been illuminated from within.

Or had his toes held to the fire.

He cleared his throat. "If I take this apprenticeship, I'll insist that your father learn an old secret."

"One that has been kept from him?" Enigma watched as Arkan nodded. "That may make him angry. I suggest you take a dragon with you for that event, so you can meet fire with fire."

Arkan found himself smiling. "Good idea. Do you know one who might be interested?"

She smiled back. "I do, especially if it means you remaining at the palace."

They stared at each other, the heat growing between them with every passing second, and Arkan couldn't think of a single reason to decline an apprenticeship with his uncle. He would train to become the viceroy of Incendium, under his own terms, and have the protection of a dragon princess, too.

He wouldn't have been the man he was if he hadn't hoped for even more.

Arkan didn't remember.

Enigma didn't know whether to be disappointed or relieved. It had been twenty years, just the blink of an eye for her, but she knew that men perceived time differently. It could have been yesterday, the memory was so clear in her mind. Arkan was more of a man than a young rebel, more concerned with convention, more responsible— more attractive.

And less drunk. That could explain a lot.

He wasn't her HeartKeeper, she knew that, and he wasn't the Carrier of the Seed for her. He was just a delicious temptation, and one that Enigma couldn't deny now any more than she'd been able to then.

When Kraw took him to her father, she couldn't stay away. She followed at a distance, blending into the shadows as she could do so well, making sure neither of the men were aware of her.

It would be more tricky to deceive her father.

But she had to know what Arkan was going to do, whether she'd see him again, whether he would be living at close proximity. She had to know whether there might be another interlude like that first one.

His children were cute, although she wasn't particularly maternal. Kraw found a maid to watch them with his usual ease of sorting out details and they seemed happy to go with her. Enigma hoped they would be similarly occupied after Arkan took up his post as Kraw's apprentice.

She slipped into the audience chamber after Kraw and Arkan, no more substantial than a ghost, and neither noticed her silent presence. Her mother was there, as were Thalina and her HeartKeeper, Acion. Thalina looked as pleased as Ignita, and Enigma guessed that they had been talking about the child she carried. Her sisters and mother always shared the same little smile when there was a young dragon on the way. Acion's hair had grown long enough to curl over his collar, though she couldn't forget his origins. He still seemed passionless to Enigma, though Thalina might be sufficiently lively for both of them.

Maybe it was true that opposites attracted.

Enigma remained back against the wall, listening as the entire story of the viceroy Narkam and his deception was explained to the king. Her father listened, a frown marring his brow, but she knew he was more puzzled than angry.

"Who was the Regalian woman?" he asked when Arkan fell silent.

"Witch," Ignita corrected.

"No witches on Incendium, Ignita," Ouros said under his breath, the words so low that Kraw gave no sign of hearing them. Arkan, however, appeared to be startled for a moment, perhaps taken aback by her father's bluntness.

"We don't know, your majesty," Arkan said. "We have only the contents of this confession for reference."

Ouros rose to his feet. "So, we don't know where Blazion and Embron went, much less whether they survived. We don't know the woman's full role, and we don't know whether she truly could bend time. They haven't come back, and neither have any of their descendants." He lifted his shoulders in a shrug. "The matter seems to be resolved."

"With respect, your majesty, it has always been anticipated that the crown would perceive my forebear's actions as treason."

"Defiance of a tyrant in the hope of saving the realm isn't my definition of treason," Ouros said mildly. "If it reassures you, I'll issue an official pardon, but I would like to keep the tale a state secret."

"Of course!"

Ouros glanced at Thalina and Acion, both of whom nodded agreement. Then he wagged a finger at the viceroy. "But here is what I want to know. The ShadowCaster showed me a vision of this incident, presumably to spark my curiosity and your confession. Why has the truth become of import now?"

"Perhaps it has taken the ShadowCaster centuries to reach your hand, sir," Arkan speculated.

"I don't think so. It was just sent to me, in quite an expedient fashion, by the Hive of Cumae. Is that the correct name, Acion?"

"It is, sir. The Hive is a sophisticated maker of androids, housed deep beneath the surface of Cumae."

Ouros nodded, evidently having been told this already. "And this Hive sent the ShadowCaster to me, after the Warrior Maiden Arista retrieved it from Regalia."

"There is no telling how long it was upon Regalia, your majesty," Kraw observed. "It could have been diverted from its destination by Queen Arcana."

"And we will never know the truth of that, now that both she and Urbanus are dead." Ouros held up a hand. "No, I have no regrets about that situation, but it does leave room for questions. Why did the Hive send the ShadowCaster to me? What interest has the Hive in the affairs of Incendium? What result did the Hive hope to provoke?"

Acion frowned in concentration. "There are myriad possibilities, sir, and it would take me some time to tabulate a list from which to calculate probabilities."

"Then you had best begin," Ouros said. "I will also need as complete a list as you can create of the Hive's capabilities and known facts about it, from which I would like you to speculate upon the obstacles the Hive might present to a party who infiltrated it."

"Father!" Thalina protested.

"And," Ouros continued. "Some suggested strategies to counter these obstacles."

Acion blinked, then nodded. Enigma had the sense he had already begun.

"The wisest strategy might be to appoint Acion a role in the landing party," Thalina suggested.

"My thoughts, exactly." Ouros turned to Arkan. "Do you mean to take the post of viceroy?"

"I do, your majesty, if it pleases you."

"It does. You have six months to learn your duties, memorize the laws of Incendium, study its protocol, and prepare to depart to Cumae as part of the diplomatic mission being dispatched to learn more about the Hive and its intentions."

"But..."

Ouros turned a sharp eye upon Arkan. "Arguing with the monarch is a poor way to begin your new responsibilities."

"I cannot go to Cumae, your majesty. I have children."

"And they will have more than adequate care in your absence. Kraw must remain here to administer the government and I will need a second of command on the mission."

"Ouros! You can't mean to lead this mission yourself!" Ignita protested, but there was no question in her tone. Enigma guessed that her mother already knew her father intended to do just that.

"I must, my dear." Ouros took Ignita's hand and pressed a kiss to its back. "I have been informed that in matters of some delicacy, I am unrivaled."

Ignita flushed. "That's not the same, Ouros..."

"But I can't delegate this and I won't. I intend to go, Ignita, and I will spend these six months in rigorous training to ensure that I am as fit as possible for the task."

Ignita's lips thinned. "And I will spend it trying to convince you to assign someone else to do it."

Their gazes locked and there was a sizzle in the air, one that promised a battle of wills. Enigma doubted that either would change the mind of the other, and guessed that they both knew as much already.

"No one tickles the belly of this dragon and evades the consequences," Ouros said with resolve. "We will convince the Hive, one way or the other, to cease its meddling in the affairs of Incendium. Are we all in agreement? In exactly six months, we depart."

Ignita sighed. "And I hope we have word of Anguissa before then." Ouros took her hand again and the others filed out of the chamber, departing to begin their assigned tasks.

Enigma followed Arkan at a distance, wondering if she could persuade him to indulge in pleasure before his departure. He had changed and was less predictable than he had been twenty years before.

More reticent.

But then he turned to look back just before he escorted Kraw into that man's apartments. When his gaze brightened, Enigma knew he had seen her. She stepped out of the shadows, as if she'd intended to do as much all along, and felt his heart skip. He smiled slowly and she smiled back, her confidence in her success growing until he turned his attention back to his uncle.

Two months, at the outside, and she would have him again.

Enigma couldn't wait.

Look for

Wyvern's Outlaw

Book 7 in the Dragons of Incendium series

The Dragons of Incendium have their own website
http://dragonsofincendium.com

Books by Deborah Cooke

Third Time Lucky
Double Trouble
One More Time
All or Nothing

Flatiron Five
Simply Irresistible
Addicted to Love
In the Midnight Hour
Some Guys Have All the Luck
Bad Case of Loving You (2019)

Secret Heart Ink
Snowbound
Spring Fever
One Hot Summer Night (2018)

For books published under Deborah's pseudonym
Claire Delacroix,
please visit:

http://delacroix.net

Deborah Cooke sold her first book in 1992, a medieval romance called **The Romance of the Rose** published under her pseudonym Claire Delacroix. Since then, she has published over fifty novels in a wide variety of sub-genres, including historical romance, contemporary romance, paranormal romance, fantasy romance, time-travel romance, women's fiction, paranormal young adult and fantasy with romantic elements. She has published under the names Claire Delacroix, Claire Cross, and Deborah Cooke. **The Beauty**, part of her successful Bride Quest series of historical romances, was her first title to land on the *New York Times* List of Bestselling Books. Her books routinely appear on other bestseller lists and have won numerous awards. In 2009, she was the writer-in-residence at the Toronto Public Library, the first time the library has hosted a residency focused on the romance genre. In 2012, she was honored to receive the Romance Writers of America's Mentor of the Year Award.

Currently, she writes paranormal romances and contemporary romances under the name Deborah Cooke. She also writes medieval romances as Claire Delacroix. Deborah lives in Canada with her husband and family, as well as far too many unfinished knitting projects.

For more information about Deborah's books, please visit her website at

http://deborahcooke.com

Milton Keynes UK
Ingram Content Group UK Ltd.
UKHW040736301024
2459UKWH00026B/92